I0591467

Treasure at the Morning Glory

A Marigold Lake Cozy Mystery - Book Eight

Reva Davenport

Marigold Lake Press

For information, please contact: **Reva Davenport**
info@revadavenport.com

Cover design by Reva Davenport

Published by: Marigold Lake Press

First Edition: 2025

For everyone who believes the smallest towns hold the biggest secrets—
and that friendship, laughter, and a good cup of coffee
can solve just about anything.

And to all the dreamers (and dogs)
who know that home isn't a place—it's a feeling.

Contents

Prologue

A Treasure in the Headlines

THE AIR IN MARIGOLD Lake carried that sweet spot between summer and fall—warm sunlight on the porch, but just enough chill to make the first mug of cider feel like an accomplishment. From her perch behind the Morning Glory's front desk, **Claire Fisher** could hear the satisfying hum of a Saturday in small-town Iowa: laughter drifting from the bakery across the street, leaves whispering against the window screens, and her Boston Terrier, Sadie, snoring from her favorite spot on the braided rug.

Claire wiped her hands on her apron and glanced at the antique clock ticking above the registration bell. "It's ten past nine, Sadie. If our influencer guest doesn't come down soon, the muffins will stage a revolt."

Sadie answered with a soft grunt that sounded suspiciously like agreement.

At that exact moment, Trudy Collins descended the staircase in full social-media splendor—curling iron curls bouncing, phone extended on a pink selfie stick, and a voice just shy of Broadway volume.

"Good morning, Morning Glory followers!" she trilled. "Today's vibe? Cozy-core chic with a side of homemade carbs!"

Claire pasted on her most professional smile. "Morning, Trudy. We have cinnamon-apple muffins and a fresh pot of—"

"Wait!" Trudy spun in a slow circle, angling her phone toward the bay window. "Can you stand by the muffins, Claire? Just, like, smile like you're welcoming autumn itself?"

Claire blinked. "I can...try?"

Sadie lifted her head, unimpressed, and gave the camera her best "this again?" face.

Click. Flash. Trudy squealed. "Perfect! You're going to go viral, Claire. Maybe not as viral as that B&B in Vermont with the ghost chef, but close."

"Great," Claire said dryly. "I've always dreamed of being second to a dead baker."

Before she could pour coffee, the front door banged open. **Barb Wetherly** bustled in wearing her usual floral prints and an expression that said she'd either discovered buried treasure or a two-for-one coupon at the grocery store.

"Have you seen the news?" Barb waved the *Marigold Gazette* like it might burst into flames. "A treasure hunt! Right here in town! Million-dollar prize, Claire! Million. With an M."

Trudy gasped theatrically, nearly dropping her phone. "Oh my gosh, say that again while I record it!"

Claire took the paper before Barb could hyperventilate. The bold headline read:

MILLION-DOLLAR TREASURE HUNT COMES TO MARIGOLD LAKE.

Below it: *Clues to be released to select recipients over the next two weeks.*

She frowned. "This has to be a publicity stunt. Marigold Lake doesn't have a million of anything except pumpkin pies."

Barb leaned in, whispering conspiratorially. "It says the first clue goes to someone called *The Keeper of Memories.* That's you, Claire! The Morning Glory has more memories stuffed in its attic than the library has books."

Claire laughed, but unease pricked at her. "That's just because I haven't cleaned the attic since last winter."

"Or," Barb said, eyes gleaming, "because fate is calling."

Trudy was already filming again. "Hashtag Keeper of Memories! Hashtag Treasure Hunt Queen!"

Claire groaned. "Please don't make that trend."

The bell over the kitchen door jingled as **Hannah Reed**, her best friend and assistant innkeeper, appeared carrying a tray of muffins and wearing a streak of flour on her cheek. "What's going on? Why is Barb vibrating?"

"Treasure hunt," Barb said. "Million dollars. The Gazette says the first clue could be here."

Hannah's eyes widened. "Do you think we'll get one? Oh, imagine if the prize is buried right under the herb garden! We'd be rich and smell like rosemary forever."

"Let's not dig up my thyme again," Claire warned. "Last time Sadie thought it was a chew toy."

Sadie wagged her nub tail, clearly unbothered by past crimes.

Trudy plopped into a dining chair, flipping open her laptop. "If I livestream our search, maybe we'll get sponsors. I already have an affiliate code for shovels."

Barb squinted. "What kind of person needs a shovel sponsorship?"

"The kind who wins," Trudy said simply.

Claire folded the newspaper and set it aside, though her mind was already spinning. A riddle addressed to "The Keeper of Memories." A treasure hunt worth a fortune. And a town where everyone—from gossips to influencers to retired magicians—would chase a headline if it meant being part of the next big thing.

She looked down at Sadie, who was now pawing at the newspaper like she'd caught a scent.

"Don't tell me you're buying into this too," Claire murmured.

Sadie barked once. Loudly.

Barb gasped. "See? Even Sadie agrees. This is destiny."

Claire sighed, pouring herself a much-needed cup of coffee. "If destiny shows up at my front door, it better bring cream and sugar."

Outside, the wind rustled through the maple trees, carrying the faintest hint of something Claire couldn't quite name—curiosity, maybe. Or trouble. In Marigold Lake, the two often arrived hand in hand.

Chapter 1

Keeper of Memories

THE AROMA OF BLUEBERRY scones mingled with the faint scent of Sadie's shampoo—a combination that perfectly summed up life at the Morning Glory: half sweet, half chaos, and entirely unpredictable.

Tuesday mornings were usually quiet but today came with a million-dollar twist.

"A treasure hunt?" Hannah's voice rose an octave as she nearly dropped an armful of towels. "An *actual* treasure hunt? Claire, we could buy glitter for life!"

I laughed, pouring coffee into my chipped blue mug. "Or we could fix the leaky roof again. Imagine—no more buckets in the hallway when it rains."

Hannah made a face. "You really know how to kill the sparkle in a girl's dream."

Barb Wetherly, perched on a kitchen stool like she owned the place, stirred her coffee with a spoon that had seen too many gossip sessions. "A million dollars, you say? If I were hiding treasure, I'd bury it under Mayor Reed's petunias. That man's secrets could fill a vault."

"Barb," I said, fighting a smile, "you can't just accuse the mayor of hoarding gold."

"I'm not accusing. I'm hypothesizing," she replied primly. "You don't buy that much fertilizer unless you're growing something—or hiding something."

Before I could respond, the morning took a strange turn.

An envelope—cream-colored, elegant, and sealed with blue wax—slid onto the counter as if dropped by invisible hands. The handwriting on the front read:

To the Keeper of Memories.

My fingers stilled around my coffee mug. "Well, that's... oddly specific."

Hannah gasped. "That's you, Claire! You *keep memories*! You run a bed-and-breakfast full of them!"

"Or it's a mix-up with the historical society's mail," I said. But the air had changed, like the walls themselves were listening.

Barb leaned closer, eyes gleaming. "Open it before I do."

I broke the seal and unfolded the note inside. The paper smelled faintly of lavender and something older—something like history.

The first clue belongs to the one who remembers.
Seek what was left beneath the ivy and pine.

I blinked. "What on earth does that mean?"

Barb gasped as if she'd just solved a cold case. "The ivy and pine! You've got both here—the south porch and the back-yard. Claire, it's a sign!"

"Or it's an elaborate prank," I countered. "You know how this town loves drama."

Sadie barked once from under the table, her nub tail wagging.

Hannah clapped her hands together. "See? Even Sadie agrees!"

"Sadie also agrees with bacon, squirrels, and anyone holding a biscuit," I reminded her.

Trudy burst in, holding her phone aloft. "Claire, you're trending!"

I froze mid-sip. "Please tell me it's for my scones."

"Better," she said, grinning. "I posted a video of Barb yelling about the treasure. It's already at twelve thousand views. The caption's *'Treasure Fever Hits Marigold Lake!'*"

Barb adjusted her scarf. "Fame suits me."

I pressed my fingers to my temple. "We're not turning the B&B into a reality show."

"Too late," Trudy said cheerfully. "Hashtag Keeper of Memories is already climbing."

3

Before I could lecture anyone about hashtags, the front door bell jingled, and a familiar voice cut through the chatter.

"Please tell me you're not planning to dig up your own porch," Detective Matt Hale said, stepping into the kitchen.

His tone was dry as toast, but his eyes held a trace of amusement.

"Not yet," I said. "But I did get this." I handed him the letter.

He scanned it, brow furrowed. "Someone's starting this treasure hunt with style."

"Or mischief," I said.

"Or both," Barb added. "Most of our town events end in both."

Matt's lips twitched, the closest he got to a smile on duty. "Just don't let the whole county dig up your garden. We're already dealing with kids tearing up park benches looking for clues."

Hannah tilted her head. "Is it true the prize is a million dollars?"

He gave a slow shrug. "That's what the Gazette says. But if you ask me, the real mystery's who's behind it. No one's claimed sponsorship."

Barb leaned in conspiratorially. "Could be government gold."

Matt deadpanned. "Or a marketing gimmick."

I folded the letter carefully. "Whatever it is, it's here now."

Outside, the wind stirred the ivy along the porch rail. The leaves whispered softly against the wood, like they knew more than we did.

Sadie's ears perked. She gave a low, curious woof.

Hannah grinned. "Looks like your assistant detective's already on the case."

I smiled despite myself. "She's probably after a snack."

Still, as I glanced again at the letter's looping script, something about it tugged at me—a quiet weight behind the words *Keeper of Memories.*

And for reasons I couldn't explain, I felt certain that whatever the treasure was, it wasn't gold we were about to uncover.

Chapter 2

The House that History Forgot

THE AUTUMN AIR NIPPED at my cheeks, painting them pink to match the berry stain on my floral apron. It wasn't my most glamorous look, but then again, sleuthing never was. Beside me, Sadie strutted proudly in her argyle sweater—a Hannah original—while Hannah herself trailed behind, phone in hand, snapping photos for her social media campaign.

"Seriously, Hannah," I said, dodging a pile of damp leaves. "Put the phone down before you fall into the lake. Then we'll have a real headline: *Local Assistant Becomes Lake Legend.*"

She giggled and pocketed the phone. "Okay, okay. But #TreasureHuntingAdventures is trending in my feed. We're practically Marigold Lake celebrities."

"Let's focus on finding a million dollars before you start signing autographs."

We turned down the narrow path leading to the old community oven—one of Marigold Lake's many relics from a time when people still thought baking bread outdoors was a good idea in Iowa weather. The brick structure crouched beneath a canopy of maple trees, its chimney leaning like it had heard one secret too many.

Sadie gave a low bark, and I didn't blame her. The scene ahead looked like something out of a small-town courtroom drama.

Mrs. Ainsworth stood stiffly in a tweed suit, using her silver letter opener to brush moss from the bricks as if single-handedly restoring civilization. Nearby, Gary Mullins—grease-stained, red-faced, and armed with a wrench—was crouched by the oven door muttering words not suitable for the church bulletin.

"Well, well, well," Mrs. Ainsworth drawled when she spotted us. "If it isn't the Morning Glory brigade. Come to poach my discovery, dear?"

"Just admiring the craftsmanship," I said.

Gary shot me a suspicious glare, his wrench still in hand. "Craftsmanship, my foot. You're all after my locket. Found it fair and square."

He held up a tarnished heart-shaped pendant like a man displaying the Holy Grail.

"Found it?" Mrs. Ainsworth sniffed. "You mean vandalized it loose with that ridiculous wrench."

"I was investigating!"

"Investigating with a wrench. How scholarly."

Sadie growled softly, and I couldn't tell if she was defending justice or just picking up on the general tension.

"Okay, everyone," I said, palms raised. "Let's dial down the drama before someone gets brained with a letter opener. We're all here for the same reason—to solve the mystery and maybe, just maybe, find the treasure."

"Speak for yourself," Gary said, clutching the locket tighter. "I'm looking for Eleanor Wexler's lost love letters. They're worth more than a million to the right collector."

That caught my attention. "Love letters?"

He nodded. "My grandpa worked for the Wexlers. Told me Eleanor's letters were hidden to protect her reputation."

Mrs. Ainsworth's eyes gleamed behind her glasses. "Eleanor Wexler and Robert Ramsey, the pharmacist. Everyone knows the story. It was the talk of the town—well, before most of the town was born."

"A pharmacist?" Hannah blinked. "That's the least romantic profession imaginable."

"On the contrary," Mrs. Ainsworth said, "he was very handsome and very attentive. Poor man never recovered after

Eleanor married Charles Wexler, the lumber baron. They say Robert died of a broken heart."

Hannah gasped. "A love triangle! This is better than the soap opera you made me watch last week."

"It was a tragedy, not a soap," Mrs. Ainsworth corrected, though the faintest smile tugged at her mouth.

Gary cleared his throat. "My grandpa said the letters—and maybe a few valuables—were hidden near this oven. The Wexlers didn't just bake bread here; they used it as a meeting place."

"Romantic and efficient," I said. "Nothing says eternal love like yeast."

Hannah snorted, earning a look from Mrs. Ainsworth.

I crouched beside the oven. The bricks were warm from the morning sun, slick with moss. Faded initials were scratched into one side: **E.W.** intertwined with **R.R.,** the lines carved deep enough to last a century.

"Eleanor Wexler and Robert Ramsey," I murmured. "They even left their mark."

"Proof," Gary said smugly. "Told you."

I examined the oven's foundation, half expecting to see the glint of gold. Instead, Sadie nosed around the edges, pawing at the dirt until something metallic flashed beneath her paw.

"Good girl," I said, brushing away the soil. A small, heart-shaped locket appeared, its surface dulled by time.

"See?" Gary exclaimed. "My locket!"

"Your raccoon-chewed locket," Mrs. Ainsworth said. "Hardly evidence of anything but bad luck."

Ignoring their squabble, I held the locket up to the light. The front bore Eleanor's initials, **E.W.**, and the back was plain. It felt heavy—almost too heavy for something so small.

"Can you open it?" Hannah asked.

"It's rusted shut." I tugged gently. Nothing.

"I've got tools," Gary offered, already rummaging through his battered toolbox. "Try this." He handed me a tiny screwdriver that looked like it had last been used on a carburetor.

"Delicate touch, please," Mrs. Ainsworth warned, clasping her pearls as if expecting an explosion.

I slid the screwdriver into the seam and twisted. The locket gave a soft click and opened.

Inside was a faded photograph: a young woman with dark curls—Eleanor Wexler—and a handsome man beside her, his hand brushing hers. The love between them radiated through the sepia tone.

"Oh my," Mrs. Ainsworth whispered. "They were beautiful."

For a moment, all of us were quiet. Even Sadie sat still, head tilted.

But there was something else inside. Tucked behind the photograph was a sliver of rolled paper, yellowed but intact.

I teased it free and unrolled it carefully. The handwriting was elegant, deliberate.

The sweetest spice hides the bitter truth.

Hannah frowned. "What does that even mean?"

I read it again, the words curling in my mind. *Sweetest spice. Bitter truth.*

Mrs. Ainsworth pursed her lips. "Sounds like another riddle. The Wexlers always were fond of theatrics."

"Or cooking," I said slowly. "Sweet spice could mean cinnamon, nutmeg, clove…"

"Or gossip," Hannah added helpfully. "That's the sweetest spice in Marigold Lake."

Gary rolled his eyes. "You all can joke, but that's a real clue. My grandpa said Eleanor used code phrases in her letters—she and Robert wrote about spices to disguise what they were saying."

Mrs. Ainsworth's brows shot up. "Are you implying she hid something in a recipe?"

"Exactly," Gary said. "A recipe, a letter, maybe even a ledger. *The sweetest spice hides the bitter truth.*"

A gust of wind carried the smell of burning leaves from somewhere down the road. The scent mingled with the faint aroma of old ashes still trapped inside the oven's hearth.

"Nutmeg," I murmured. "Aunt Teresa used to say nutmeg was her favorite spice—'sweet enough to comfort, strong enough to bite back.' She got that from an old Wexler cookbook."

Hannah brightened. "So, the next clue's in a recipe?"

"Maybe," I said. "Or somewhere connected to it. We should check Aunt Teresa's cookbook when we get back."

Gary clutched the empty locket. "Hey, I found that fair and square. What about me?"

"You can come to the B&B for pie," I said. "But the clue's coming with me."

Mrs. Ainsworth gave a satisfied nod. "A wise choice, dear. You're far more equipped to handle delicate history than Mr. Mullins and his wrench."

Gary sputtered something about "ungrateful amateurs," but by then Sadie was tugging me toward the path.

As we walked back toward the lake, Hannah tucked the folded clue into her pocket for safekeeping. "So what do you think the bitter truth is?" she asked.

"Something the Wexlers wanted buried," I said. "Love, money, reputation—take your pick. But the sweetest spice? That's a recipe for trouble."

Sadie barked twice, tail wagging, as if agreeing that trouble was her favorite course.

Behind us, the voices of Mrs. Ainsworth and Gary drifted through the trees—bickering about who had rightful claim to Marigold history. Typical.

We crossed the footbridge over the creek, the afternoon sun glinting through the trees. Hannah's phone buzzed again, and she groaned. "It's Barb. She wants to know if we've unearthed the treasure or just more gossip."

"Tell her both," I said. "It's Marigold Lake—we never get one without the other."

Sadie leapt into the passenger seat when we reached the car, leaving a perfect set of muddy paw prints on my apron to commemorate the day. I didn't even bother wiping them off.

"Next stop," I said, starting the engine, "Aunt Teresa's cookbook. Let's see which spice in her pantry hides a scandal."

As we pulled away, the locket glinted once in Hannah's hand, catching the sunlight. Inside, the young couple smiled eternally, their secret waiting just beneath the surface.

The sweetest spice hides the bitter truth.

Whatever Eleanor Wexler had meant by those words, I had a feeling they were about to flavor our investigation—and not in the comforting, cinnamon-roll kind of way.

Chapter 3

The Wexler Waltz

"A WEXLER SCANDAL?" I echoed, stirring my rapidly cooling coffee. After the pie-filling fiasco and the unnerving discovery of Eleanor Wexler's locket, caffeine felt less like a luxury and more like a life requirement.

Nanette Caldwell perched on the edge of the floral armchair like a hummingbird about to bolt, her eyes gleaming behind her spectacles. Sunlight poured through the Morning Glory's bay window, catching the dust motes swirling around her like tiny conspirators.

Outside, Marigold Lake glowed in its autumn costume—scarlets and golds reflected in the rippling water. Normally, the scent of burning leaves drifting in from Main Street would have wrapped me in cozy contentment. Today, it just made my stomach twist.

"Oh, honey, Marigold Lake's got more scandals than it does squirrels," Nanette said, voice sweet as tea but sharp as nutmeg. "And that's saying something. You know how many squirrels raid Mrs. Abernathy's bird feeders? The woman's waging a one-person war."

Sadie, who never missed a good story, abandoned her nap on the rug and padded over to Nanette, planting herself squarely at her feet. Nanette reached down to scratch behind her ears. "Good girl. Always ready for gossip. Just like your mama."

Sadie snorted in agreement, her tail nub thumping the floor.

"So, what happened?" Hannah asked, leaning forward on the settee with a gleam in her eyes that could rival polished silver. Subtlety, as usual, was not in her skill set.

Nanette gave a satisfied hum, adjusting her scarf. "Back in the day, the Wexlers were practically royalty around here. Owned half the lumber mills, threw parties that put city galas to shame. They were the Vanderbilts of Marigold Lake—only with more flannel and fewer yachts."

I smiled. "And, I assume, just as dramatic?"

"Oh, of course. But the fall—now, that was something." Nanette's tone dropped to a storyteller's whisper. "One day, the family was hosting lavish dinners; the next, they were selling the drapes to pay their debts. Rumors flew thicker than gnats in July. Embezzlement, gambling, a secret love child—you name it, people whispered it."

"Secret love child?" Hannah gasped. "Ooh, maybe they're the one behind the treasure hunt! Coming back to reclaim their fortune!"

I shot her a look. "We're solving a mystery, not writing a soap opera. Though, admittedly, *Secrets and Scones* would make a good title."

Nanette chuckled, the sound like leaves rustling across the porch. "Don't give anyone ideas. But the truth was stranger than gossip ever managed. The Wexler fortune vanished overnight. Old Man Hemlock claimed he saw Reginald Wexler sneaking out of town with a suitcase of cash and a woman who wasn't his wife. Then again, Hemlock also swore Elvis worked at the Dairy Queen, so we take his testimony with sprinkles."

Sadie sneezed, possibly in disbelief.

"So what actually happened?" I asked. "We've got clues popping up faster than Hannah's hashtags, but none of them tell the whole story."

Nanette folded her hands in her lap, expression turning serious. "There were lawsuits. Accusations. The family was torn apart. Some Wexlers left town entirely. The ones who stayed faded into quiet shame. They went from grand balls to quiet funerals in just a few years."

"A love child, missing inheritance, vanished fortune..." Hannah's eyes sparkled. "Maybe the treasure is the inheritance. Maybe the locket we found belonged to that child."

I rolled my eyes, though her theory wasn't entirely off the table. "If the treasure turns out to be old jewelry and scandal, I'm demanding hazard pay."

Nanette leaned forward. "The key detail, dear, is the Wexler Waltz. That was the final gala the family hosted—a grand masquerade in the old town hall, the night before everything went wrong. Some say the fortune—and the truth—disappeared that same evening."

"The Wexler Waltz," I repeated, the words rolling like the title of a tragic ballad. "That's what the clue mentioned. But why the town hall? These days it's mostly a graveyard for tinsel and outdated tax files."

Nanette smiled faintly. "Every town keeps its ghosts somewhere, Claire. Ours just happen to share storage space with the Christmas garland."

Before I could ask more, Sadie's head popped up, ears perked. A moment later, the bell over the front door chimed.

Matt Hale stepped inside, bringing a swirl of crisp air with him. His coat was damp with dew, his hair slightly mussed, and his expression somewhere between concern and irritation—the look of a man who'd been chasing trouble before breakfast.

"Everything okay?" I asked, my heart doing a small, traitorous skip.

"Not exactly." He scanned the room: Nanette, seated like a queen with secrets; Hannah, practically bouncing with curiosity; and Sadie, who'd already trotted over to greet him with her usual full-body wag.

He rubbed her head absently. "Gary Mullins called. Someone tampered with the brakes on his truck last night. He nearly plowed into Mrs. Ainsworth's petunias."

"Again?" I said.

"Again," Matt confirmed. "But this time it wasn't user error. The line was cut."

Hannah's jaw dropped. "Cut, like... *sabotage* cut?"

"Looks that way."

Nanette clicked her tongue. "Good heavens. First love letters, now attempted vehicular manslaughter. Marigold Lake's really outdoing itself this fall."

Matt gave a humorless half-smile. "I think someone's taking this treasure hunt a little too seriously."

I folded my arms. "Or they don't want anyone getting too close to the truth."

His eyes met mine—gray-blue and stormy. "That's what worries me. You've been poking around long enough that someone might see you as a threat."

Hannah gave a nervous laugh. "She's fine. She's got Sadie and a rolling pin."

Sadie barked once, as if confirming her status as both body-guard and carb consultant.

Matt's voice softened. "Just... be careful, Claire. I'm not convinced this is about money anymore."

"I never was," I said quietly.

Nanette sighed. "These things have a way of repeating, dear. Greed, jealousy, pride—they don't fade, they just change names."

Outside, the wind picked up, rattling the porch wind chimes in a melancholy tune.

"I think the next clue's tied to that last ball," I said finally. "The Wexler Waltz. Whatever happened that night—it started everything."

Matt nodded slowly. "Then that's where we start digging. Carefully."

Sadie gave another decisive bark, her tail thumping against the door like a gavel.

Nanette smiled wryly. "She's right, you know. Every good mystery starts with a dance. Let's just hope this one doesn't end in disaster."

I glanced down at the locket on the table, its tarnished surface catching the light. Somewhere between its two halves lay a story of love, loss, and betrayal—and, apparently, sabotage.

Marigold Lake's secrets were stirring again, and it looked like we'd just stepped onto the dance floor.

Chapter 4

Sugar, Spice, and a Suspicious Nutmeg

THE SECOND CLUE ARRIVED tucked inside a Betty Crocker cookbook, wedged between "Deviled Ham Spread" and "Easy Scalloped Potatoes." Aunt Teresa's Betty Crocker, to be exact—the one with the cracking spine, dog-eared pages, and a faint aura of vanilla that clung to it like a lovesick suitor. It felt intimate, like she was still guiding me from beyond the veil. Except this time, instead of advising me to reduce heat before a boil-over, she appeared to be leading me toward a fortune and a headache.

"Well, that's just... creepy," Hannah said, leaning over my shoulder so close her ponytail tickled my ear. She jerked back, nearly tripping over Sadie, who had stationed herself in optimal crumb-catching position. "How did they even know about Aunt Teresa's cookbook? I thought it was our secret stash."

Sadie went in for a lick. I slid the book away. "Bad Sadie. No tasting potential evidence."

The index card itself had been tucked neatly behind the plastic sleeve that held Aunt Teresa's handwritten conversions. Purple ink—grandma-stationery purple—looped into a rhyme:

Where sugar and spice meet a family's plight,
A secret ingredient hides in plain sight.*
Seek the recipe whispered on bended knee,*
The Wexler fortune's key, for all to see.*

I read it twice. The second time, it snagged in my chest. This wasn't just a scavenger hunt anymore; it was personal. Sugar and spice. A whispered recipe. A family's plight. It tangled Wexler history with the Morning Glory's beating heart—our kitchen.

"Okay, officially freaked out," I announced, slapping the cookbook onto the island with a thud. Sadie yipped at the noise, then snorted like she'd been arguing the same thing for minutes.

Matt pushed off the doorframe where he'd been lurking, arms crossed, expression unreadable. In jeans and a slate T-shirt, he was very much off duty and still somehow the most detective-y person in the room. He took the card, scanned it, and set it back down. "Messing with you," he said. "Specifically you. 'Keeper of Memories,' the cookbook, this rhyme. Whoever this is? They know your soft spots."

"Fun observation. Thank you," I said, but I didn't snap. Not quite. He had that "I warned you" crease between his eyebrows. I hated that crease.

Hannah tapped her chin, eyes bright. "Well, if we're talking sugar-and-spice recipes Aunt Teresa whispered like a church secret... Morning Glory Muffins." She clasped her hands. "They're basically the official breakfast of Marigold Lake."

I pulled the book around, flipped to Teresa's typed insert—pasted over Betty Crocker's base recipe years ago—and scanned the list. Flour, brown sugar, crushed pineapple, grated carrot, cinnamon, raisins, walnuts. Butter. Eggs. Vanilla. The choir of breakfast angels.

Matt peered over my shoulder. "Nothing secret about that."

"Unless the secret is hiding in plain sight." I traced the ingredients again. A memory stirred; Aunt Teresa's laugh, the playful twirl of her spoon before she tapped nutmeg over the bowl "for luck." "She used to say one spice was the soul of the batter. A pinch and a prayer."

Hannah leaned closer. "Which one?"

Sadie answered for us, nosing the page insistently and thunking her nub tail against the cabinet like a metronome.

Her nose smudged a faint paw-shaped mark right over a line I'd skimmed twice already:

1 teaspoon freshly grated nutmeg.

"Nutmeg?" Hannah deflated. "That's it? *The sweetest spice hides the bitter truth,* and it's... nutmeg? I mean, it's nice, but it's not exactly a treasure-map spice."

"Maybe it's not what," Matt said. "Maybe it's where. Did Teresa have a source?"

"She had sources for everything," I murmured. "Lavender from a woman who swore bees spoke to her in Latin, honey from a beekeeper who never used words under five syllables, and eggs from chickens she insisted were 'philosophical.'" I lifted the book, the old paper soft against my fingers. "There was a Founder's Day bake sale years ago—she said she'd gotten 'exotic' nutmeg for a special batch. Folks were nearly elbowing each other for them."

"Exotic from where?" Hannah's voice had recovered, hope returning on a sugar high. "Sri Lanka? Zanzibar? Did it arrive in a tiny velvet pouch with a map tied in twine?"

"I don't know. She never told me." I closed my eyes for a beat. "But she made a trip that week... I remember the muddy tires." The memory sharpened, a Polaroid developing. "She drove out toward Willow Creek Farm."

"Old Man Hemlock," Barb said as she breezed into the kitchen with the speed and subtlety of a gust through a wind chime. She set down a paper sack that smelled suspiciously like cinnamon pretzels. "I heard you invoke nutmeg thrice, so I came running."

"Were you eavesdropping?" I asked.

"Of course," she said cheerfully. "And yes, Hemlock. He's got herbs and spices tucked all over that place. He sold at the farmers' market before it became solely kettle corn and ironic pickles."

Hannah wrinkled her nose. "Hemlock gives me the willies. He always looks like he knows when you last flossed."

"He's odd," I conceded. "But not dangerous. Just... earnest dirt." I glanced at the card again. "If Teresa bought nutmeg from him before Founder's Day, maybe that's our thread."

Matt's mouth flattened. "Or it's bait. Don't go alone."

"Wasn't planning to." I grabbed my keys. "Come on, Sadie. Time to sniff the spice trail."

Sadie bounded for the door, skidding slightly on the runner like a cartoon character. Hannah snatched the cookbook and index card, tucked both into a tote bag, and followed. Barb grabbed the paper sack.

I looked back at Matt. He was watching me with that mix of concern and resignation I'd come to recognize as *accepting the inevitable*. I lifted a shoulder. "You could call Hemlock and ruin my day. Or you could come and ruin it in person."

He sighed. "I'll follow. If he chases you out with a trowel, I'm not wrestling him."

"Please," Hannah said, already halfway to the door. "You'd win. His superpower is being dusty."

We piled into the Mini Cooper—Hannah up front, Sadie in the back on her blanket throne—and pulled out. In the rearview mirror, Matt's cruiser slid onto the road behind us, a steady shadow.

Willow Creek Farm lay beyond town where the road narrowed, the lake's glimmer giving way to fields and a thin stand of trees. The driveway was a suggestion rather than a surface, more ruts and grasses than gravel. A red barn squatted near a tilting farmhouse whose porch sagged like it was tired of holding secrets. Beyond the barn, a long low greenhouse stretched along the hedgerow, its panes fogged from the inside.

"Picturesque," Hannah said. "If your aesthetic is *haunted spice merchant.*"

Sadie let out a soft woof, the kind that meant this place smelled interesting. I patted her head. "You're on point today; keep it professional."

We were halfway to the porch when the door creaked open and Old Man Hemlock appeared. He wasn't as ancient as legend made him—seventies, maybe—but he had the air of a person time forgot to collect. Corduroy jacket, garden-stained cuffs, and a gray beard that looked as if it only consented to trimming under legal duress. His eyes, though—sharp and pale, like winter sky.

"Caldwell's girls," he said, which startled me; no one had put me and Aunt Teresa in the same basket of girls in years. Then he clocked Matt climbing out of the cruiser and added, "And the law." His gaze dropped to Sadie. "And a T-rex."

"Boston Terrier," I said. "Jurassic lineage aside."

He smiled, barely. "Teresa's mutt had better manners."

"She did," I admitted. "And she also had a taste for nutmeg."

"You don't say." He opened the door wider. "Well, that tracks."

We stepped into a hallway that smelled like potting soil and cloves. Jars lined a high shelf, each labeled in Hemlock's neat hand: star anise, long pepper, bay, cassia, mace. A kettle hissed somewhere toward the back.

Hannah whispered, "This is my dream pantry," then caught herself and added, "For legal spices."

Hemlock led us to the kitchen and waved at chairs. "Tea?" Without waiting for an answer, he set out mugs. "Teresa was fond of Assam," he said, and my throat tightened in that traitor way memory still gets you—in the soft spots when you're busy pretending to be hard.

"We're actually here about that," I said when the kettle clicked off. "Teresa bought nutmeg from you once. The week of the Founder's Day bake sale."

He didn't bother with the acting; he only nodded like he'd been expecting this. "Everyone wanted that nutmeg after her muffins. Sold out of it in two days."

"You had whole nuts?" I asked. "She grated it fresh."

"Had a shipment of *Myristica fragrans* and a little *Myristica malabarica*," he said, as if reciting the weather. "The latter's fiercer. Teresa liked the bite."

Hannah blinked. "Translation for those of us who do not moonlight as wizards?"

"Nutmeg, two types," I said. "One sweeter, one with bark." I glanced at Hemlock. "Do you still have any?"

He tipped his head toward the greenhouse. "Not in here."

We followed him back outside. Up close, the greenhouse glass wore a lace of condensation. Inside, the air was warm and layered with perfume—earth, citrus peel, the licorice wink of fennel, the lemony brightness of dried verbena. Jars lined sturdy wooden benches; in the far corner, a small steel locker rested against the wall.

Hemlock unlocked it and set a shallow wooden box on the bench: whole nutmeg wrapped in paper, like a tray of dark marbles. He slid one parcel forward with a knuckle. "From the old lot. Kept a few aside for seed stock. Teresa's came from the same crate."

Hannah breathed, "They're pretty," like she'd found a clutch of gemstones.

I picked one up. It had weight to it, the shell firm and faintly ridged. I could almost see Teresa at her counter, tapping the grater, the aroma lifting off the batter like secrets at dawn.

"Mind if I...?" I asked.

Hemlock waved me on. I took a paring knife from a bench caddy and shaved the merest sliver. The scent rose—a warm, woody sweetness with that peppered edge that made your tongue want to chase it. Grief and comfort in one breath.

"That's the one," I said, and set it down.

Sadie, who had been snuffling like a sommelier at a tasting, nosed under the bench and sneezed herself backward, then put a paw against the locker. Tap, tap. Paw again. Tap.

"Subtle," Matt murmured from the doorway. He hadn't come in far—police habit—but he watched everything.

I crouched and felt under the locker. My fingertips brushed something that didn't belong—a small cylinder taped against the underside. I peeled it free. It was a whole nutmeg, but as I rolled it in my palm, the balance felt wrong.

"Hollow," Hemlock said, as if I'd rediscovered a trick he'd heard about in a song. "Been a long time since I've seen that."

"With what inside?" Hannah breathed.

"Only one way to find out." I glanced at Hemlock. He shrugged. I wrapped the nut loosely in a scrap of paper, tapped it with the handle of the knife, and the shell split along a neat seam, more like a cleverly made bead than a seed. Inside lay a curl of parchment no wider than a fingernail.

I teased it open, careful as a jeweler. The ink had browned to sepia; the script was practiced, upright, and heavy on flourishes. Not Teresa's hand. Older. Beneath a single initial—**E.**—a line:

Dance where the floor remembers.

Under it, a date I knew from Nanette's stories even if I hadn't lived it: **October 18, 1963.**

Hannah put a hand over her mouth. "The Wexler Waltz."

Matt exhaled. "Town hall."

I felt the thrill and chill that come together when mystery taps your shoulder.

Chapter 5

Secrets Beneath the Stage

BACK AT THE CAR, the sky had gentled into the pale blue that comes before afternoon turns thoughtful. Barb texted three times in five minutes—**WHERE ARE YOU / DID YOU FIND GOLD / PETUNIAS SAFE**—and I answered with a picture of the parchment and the words **town hall**.

On the way, Hannah dug into the paper sack. "Cinnamon pretzel?" she offered.

"I thought you were saving those for stress emergencies," I said.

She tore one in half and handed me a piece. "We are in a stress emergency. Also I didn't eat lunch."

Matt's cruiser kept its polite distance behind us, steady, dependable. The closer we drove toward Main Street, the more the town hall's brick façade rose like a memory: the columns in need of paint, the big wooden doors, the banner hooks that still held scraps of tape from festivals past. I parked along the side lot where the maples hung their lowest branches.

Inside, it was cooler, the air tasting faintly of paper and lemon oil. Chairs stacked to the ceiling, a stage that had seen more talent shows than turkeys on Rigsby's Thanksgiving table, and a floor that creaked like an old friend's knees. I stood in the center and listened.

Dance where the floor remembers.

"What are we listening for?" Hannah whispered, as if a hush would help the boards confess.

"Not listening," I said, and put my palms against my thighs to ground myself. "Feeling."

I walked slowly toward the west side, where the stage cast a long wood shadow in afternoons. The fourth plank from the edge, halfway down, gave a whisper of difference: not louder, just... hollower. I pressed my heel; the sound thudded, then answered itself with a faint echo.

"Here," I said.

Matt was already kneeling, running his fingertips along the seam where two boards met. "There's a hairline," he said. He took a small penlight from his pocket, angled it, and nodded. "Trap strip."

Hannah bounced on her toes. "Like a speakeasy!"

"Like a maintenance access," Matt corrected, but his voice had that thread of excitement I recognized when puzzles started behaving.

We didn't have tools. We had initiative and a bobby pin Hannah produced from thin air, because of course she did. With a little coaxing, the strip lifted, and a narrow rectangle of darkness opened like a breath. Cold air rose out, carrying the faint scent of cedar and something older, like locked paper.

"Don't stick your hand in," Matt said as I leaned. "Please."

"I'm not reckless," I said, and to prove it, I took my phone flashlight and aimed a beam into history.

At the bottom of the shallow cavity sat a tin no bigger than a recipe card box. Green enamel, worn to silver at the edges, with a white heart painted on the lid—the same heart we'd found in Cabin Nine. I swallowed.

"Okay," Hannah breathed. "This is definitely the right floor."

Matt slid his fingertips into the gap and lifted the tin with surgeon care. Dust arced up, caught in the light, then settled like quiet applause. He set the box on a folding table, glanced at me, and raised a brow that asked the question he didn't voice: *Ready?*

"As I'll ever be," I said, and opened it.

Inside, on top, lay a dance card from the Wexler Waltz, the paper still surprisingly stiff. Names written in a neat hand—some familiar, some lost to time. Under it: a folded letter sealed with brittle wax impressed with a **W.** And beneath that, wrapped in oilcloth, something rigid and rectangular like a ledger spine.

We didn't move. For a heartbeat, even Sadie stopped breathing.

Then somewhere out in the hallway, a floorboard popped—an ordinary building sound, probably, except that it sounded like a footstep.

Matt's head snapped up. His eyes met mine. "Someone else is in the building," he said softly.

And just like that, nutmeg and waltzes gave way to adrenaline. I closed the tin gently, as if that might keep the room from hearing my heart. Matt angled toward the doorway, hand near his belt—instinct more than need; he wasn't carrying.

"Back of the stage," I whispered to Hannah, motioning with my chin. "There's a side door. If we need it."

The boards murmured again, closer this time.

"Claire," Matt said without looking back, "stay with me."

"Not a speck of heroics," I promised, and slid the tin carefully into my tote, tucking the strap across my body like it might anchor me to sense.

Sadie stood at my heel, shoulders squared, a tiny sentinel.

Dance where the floor remembers, the clue had said.

Apparently, we weren't the only ones who did.

Chapter 6

Secrets in the Stacks

THE MARIGOLD LAKE HISTORICAL Society was exactly what you'd expect from a place that hadn't been dusted since the Nixon administration. The air carried the faint scent of lemon polish, mildew, and secrets. Rows of mismatched filing cabinets lined one wall, each groaning under the weight of folders labeled in shaky handwriting. The front counter was buried beneath newspapers, index cards, and a coffee mug that proclaimed, **History Buffs Do It Chronologically.**

Leona Brandt looked up as Matt and I stepped through the door. Her expression landed somewhere between suspicion and mild annoyance—the look of someone whose quiet afternoon had just been interrupted by people with questions.

"Claire Fisher," she said, adjusting her bifocals. "And Detective Hale. Don't tell me the treasure hunt has turned into a crime scene already."

"Not yet," Matt said, his tone dry. "But we're trying to keep it that way."

Leona set down her pen. "You'll forgive me if I don't hold my breath."

I smiled as disarmingly as possible. "We were hoping you could help us fill in a few blanks about the Wexlers. Nanette told us the family hosted a big event here decades ago—the Wexler Waltz. Does that ring a bell?"

Leona's eyes sharpened. "It does. And it usually means trouble when it does." She gestured toward a side door. "Come on, then. If we're going to dig up old ghosts, we might as well do it properly."

The back room looked like a library and a thrift shop had collided. Stacks of bound ledgers, maps, and black-and-white photographs covered the long oak table in the center. A single desk lamp cast a yellow halo—the only light in the dim space. Dust motes drifted lazily through the beam like slow-motion snow.

Leona pulled a box labeled **Wexler – 1950–1970** from the shelf and dropped it onto the table with a thunk. "You're not the first to ask about them," she said. "Every few years, someone comes sniffing around. Usually reporters. Occasionally family. None of them stick around long."

"Why not?" I asked.

She gave a thin smile. "Because the Wexlers don't like being remembered."

I exchanged a look with Matt. "We're not exactly planning a feature article," I said. "We found something that seems to tie into the family. A locket, some letters, and a clue referencing the Wexler Waltz."

At that, Leona froze for just a fraction of a second before busying herself with the box lid. "The Waltz," she said quietly. "The night everything ended."

Hannah—who had insisted on tagging along despite my better judgment—leaned closer. "Ended how? Like, dramatic-scandal ended or fade-into-obscurity ended?"

Leona shot her a look over her glasses. "The kind of ended where people stopped using the family name."

That silenced even Hannah for a moment.

Matt folded his arms. "We found a letter sealed with a 'W' at the town hall. Still unopened. Any idea who might've written it?"

Leona hesitated, then opened a folder and pulled out a sepia-toned photograph. It showed the town hall ballroom, filled with people in formal dress. In the foreground stood Eleanor Wexler—recognizable from the locket's photograph—smiling up at a man who wasn't her husband.

"That's Robert Ramsey," Leona said softly. "The pharmacist. The one she was rumored to love."

The room seemed to exhale, the silence stretching. I felt a twinge of sympathy for Eleanor—the kind that comes when you realize the past's tragedies were once someone's Tuesdays.

"What happened that night?" I asked.

Leona rested both hands on the table, fingers splayed like she was bracing herself. "The Wexlers were already in trouble. Money issues, bad investments, and Reginald's gambling. The Waltz was meant to distract from all that—to remind everyone they were still the ruling family of Marigold Lake. But instead, it exposed them."

She flipped to another photograph: a newspaper clipping showing police cars parked outside the town hall, flashbulbs exploding.

SCANDAL AT WEXLER BALL – FAMILY FORTUNE MISSING.

"By morning," she said, "the accounts were empty. The lumber contracts were gone. And Eleanor's husband vanished along with the bookkeeper. Some said he ran off with the money. Others said he buried it. Either way, the Wexler Waltz was the last dance anyone in that family ever had."

Sadie, who had been lying under the table, let out a small, sympathetic whine, as if mourning the lost fortune.

"So the treasure could be the missing funds," Hannah said, eyes wide. "That's what all this is about!"

"Maybe," Leona said. "Or maybe it's about the truth of what really happened. Money's just the surface of things like this. It's the secrets underneath that rot everything."

I nodded slowly, feeling that familiar flutter in my chest—the one that came when the mystery started to line up, just enough to make sense and just enough to be dangerous.

Matt leaned forward, tapping the corner of the photo. "Do you remember who else was at the ball?"

"Oh, I remember plenty," Leona said. "Half the town was there. And everyone remembers one thing differently. But there's one constant. After midnight, the music stopped. The lights flickered, and Reginald Wexler made a toast. Something about legacies and new beginnings. Then there was shouting in the hallway. By the time anyone went to look, he was gone."

"Gone?" I repeated.

"Gone," she confirmed. "Left his wife standing alone in front of the orchestra."

The image sent a chill through me—the ballroom, the lights, the stunned silence. A woman clutching her pearls while her world collapsed around her.

Leona closed the folder with finality. "That's all I know. Or rather, all I can prove. The rest is rumor."

"What kind of rumor?" I asked.

Her gaze flicked to Matt, then back to me. "That Reginald didn't run off at all. That he was helped out of town—or out of this world—by someone who stood to gain from his disappearance."

Matt's jaw tightened. "Any names?"

"Plenty," she said. "None that would make you any friends."

I sighed. "This treasure hunt just keeps getting cheerier."

Leona smiled faintly. "You didn't come here for cheer. You came for answers. But be careful, Claire. The Wexlers might be gone, but their story still has teeth."

Her words lingered as we left the building. Outside, the wind had picked up, scattering a swirl of gold leaves across the steps.

"Well," Hannah said, stuffing her hands into her jacket pockets, "that was uplifting."

Matt stopped beside his car. "She's not wrong. Someone's using this treasure hunt to dig up a past the town's been trying to forget. And they're using you to do it."

I looked down at Sadie, who was busy sniffing an especially interesting patch of grass. "At least I'm in good company."

"Claire," he said softly. "You don't have to keep doing this."

I met his eyes. "You know me better than that."

He sighed, resigned. "That's what worries me."

We drove back toward town in companionable silence—the kind of quiet that hummed with unspoken thoughts. The sun dipped lower, turning the lake into a sheet of copper. Somewhere between the ripples and reflections, I caught my own face in the glass—determined, curious, a little too eager for answers.

When we pulled into the Morning Glory's gravel drive, Barb was waiting on the porch, arms crossed and a mug of tea steaming beside her.

"Well?" she called. "Find anything interesting, or just more people who talk in riddles?"

"Both," I said.

"Figures." She took a sip. "You've got mail, by the way. Some courier dropped it off while you were gone. Fancy envelope. Smells like perfume and regret."

That got my attention. I took the envelope from the railing—heavy ivory paper, my name written in the same elegant calligraphy as before.

To the Keeper of Memories.

My heart skipped.

"What does it say?" Hannah asked, peering over my shoulder.

I tore it open carefully. Inside was a single sheet of parchment, the same purple ink curling across the page:

When the heart is hollow and the waltz is done,

Seek the story beneath the sun.*

At dawn's first light where angels rest,*

The truth will rise when peace is blessed.*

"The cemetery again," Matt murmured.

"Looks that way."

Barb let out a low whistle. "You sure you're not starring in some gothic novel, Claire? Because this is getting spooky."

"Tell me about it," I said, folding the letter and sliding it into my pocket. "Looks like our next dance is with the dead."

Sadie barked once, as if to say she'd already called dibs on being lead detective.

Matt glanced toward the horizon where the sun was sinking behind the church steeple. "Then we'd better get some rest. Dawn comes early."

I nodded, though sleep was the last thing on my mind. Somewhere beneath Marigold Lake's golden glow, the Wexler story was stirring again—and I had the sinking feeling that by the time we unearthed it, we'd all be changed.

Chapter 7

Dawn Among the Angels

THE MORNING AIR HAD the bite of an apple left too long on the counter—crisp, sharp, and just a little sad. Mist clung to the ground in thin ribbons, swirling around the headstones like ghosts too polite to interrupt.

I pulled my coat tighter and glanced at the sky. The sun was still shy, just a faint wash of pink along the lake's far edge. "Well," I murmured, "someone wanted us up early."

Hannah yawned beside me, clutching a travel mug the size of a toddler. "I don't function before nine. If there's a ghost, it better hand me a latte."

Sadie trotted ahead, her stubby legs moving with determination. Her breath puffed in tiny clouds, the visible sign of her enthusiasm. She paused to sniff the base of a weathered angel statue, tail wagging in slow, deliberate circles.

"That's our first suspect," I said, crouching beside her. "Looks like the angels rest right here."

The Morning Glory's sign still glowed faintly in the distance down the hill, and the rest of Marigold Lake slumbered under a haze of fog. Matt's cruiser idled nearby, its headlights cutting through the mist like steady beacons.

He stepped out, hands shoved in his jacket pockets. "I can't believe I let you talk me into investigating a cemetery before sunrise."

"Technically, you volunteered," I said. "You just didn't realize it at the time."

He arched an eyebrow. "I said I'd bring backup, not a picnic party."

Behind him, Barb appeared carrying a thermos and two paper bags. "Speak for yourself. I brought muffins. The living still need sustenance."

"Morning Glory muffins," I guessed.

"Of course. And a splash of courage," Barb said, holding up her travel mug like a toast. "Half coffee, half Irish cream."

Matt sighed, though a smile tugged at the corner of his mouth. "You people are going to get me fired."

Hannah took a muffin and tore it in half, handing a piece to Sadie. "If this treasure hunt doesn't pan out, we could always sell these as emotional support pastries."

"Focus, team," I said, holding up the latest clue. "'At dawn's first light where angels rest, the truth will rise when peace is blessed.'" I looked toward the row of statues that bordered the older section of the cemetery. Most were angels, some missing wings, others leaning precariously after decades of Iowa winters.

"'Peace is blessed,'" Hannah said. "Sounds like the chapel."

"Maybe," I said. "But 'truth will rise' feels like... something buried."

Matt joined me beside Sadie. "Or someone. You're sure you want to dig into this, Claire?"

"Not literally," I said, though the idea didn't seem quite so figurative now.

The Marigold Cemetery wasn't large—twenty rows of graves, some so old the names had eroded away, their stories lost to wind and rain. I walked slowly between the markers, scanning for anything that stood out. The damp grass soaked through my sneakers.

The angel Sadie had stopped at earlier caught my attention again. It stood on a pedestal, wings outstretched, face tilted skyward in an expression that looked equal parts sorrow and hope. The inscription at the base read: **Eleanor Wexler, 1919–1968. Forever Loved, Forever Lost.**

My breath caught. "Eleanor," I whispered.

Hannah leaned closer. "You're kidding."

Matt crouched beside the base. "No kidding. It's her grave."

Barb's voice softened. "Guess that answers the question about whether she stayed in town."

Sadie pawed at the grass near the headstone, letting out a low bark. I knelt beside her, brushing away dew. The soil looked freshly disturbed—not by an animal, but like someone had recently dug here and replaced the sod with care.

"Matt," I said quietly.

He was already beside me, his flashlight angled down. "That's too neat to be natural."

"Could be maintenance," Hannah offered weakly.

"Or it could be our clue."

I pressed my fingers into the dirt. Cold and damp. The soil gave easily, and something metallic scraped against my nail. I dug carefully until the edge of a small box appeared—a tin about the size of a jewelry case, tarnished and half-covered in moss.

"Well, I'll be," Barb murmured. "Either that's the world's smallest time capsule or someone really wanted to give the worms a challenge."

Matt helped lift it free, brushing off dirt with the precision of a man used to evidence bags. The box creaked when I eased the lid open. Inside was a folded piece of parchment and a small brass key—its head shaped like a heart.

"The heart again," I said softly.

Hannah peered over my shoulder. "Please tell me it doesn't open a coffin."

I ignored her and unfolded the parchment. The ink was the same purple, curling in graceful loops:

To those who seek what's lost to time,

Follow where the bells still chime.*

One heart unlocks what two concealed,*

The truth once buried shall be revealed.*

Matt took the note and read it silently, jaw tightening. "The bells. That's the chapel, all right."

"'One heart unlocks what two concealed,'" I murmured. "Eleanor and Robert Ramsey. Maybe something they hid together."

"Or something someone hid from them," Barb said darkly. "Families like the Wexlers didn't get rich by being honest."

A gust of wind rattled the trees, sending leaves skittering across the graves like whispers. For a moment, the entire cemetery seemed to hold its breath.

Matt closed the box and stood. "All right. Let's head to the chapel. Before this place starts to feel too welcoming."

The chapel sat at the far edge of the cemetery, its white paint faded to cream and its bell tower leaning just enough to make you nervous. Inside, it smelled of candle wax, dust, and lilies that had given up sometime last week. Sunlight filtered through stained glass, scattering shards of color across the wooden pews.

Sadie's nails clicked softly as she padded up the aisle, nose twitching.

"Looks like no one's been here in a while," Hannah whispered.

"Except whoever left that box," I said.

Matt swept his flashlight across the walls, pausing on a plaque near the altar: **Dedicated to the Memory of the Wexler Family, 1965.**

"Fitting," Barb said. "They've managed to haunt both sides of town."

I approached the altar, the brass key cool in my palm. It wasn't like the others we'd found—this one had an engraving along the side: **RR + EW.**

"Robert and Eleanor," I murmured.

Hannah leaned over my shoulder. "A heart-shaped key for a heart-shaped mess."

Sadie barked once, sharp and insistent. She was staring at the old wooden lectern. Beneath it, a small metal keyhole glinted.

"Well, that's convenient," I said.

Matt crouched, brushing away dust. "Looks like it hasn't been used in decades."

"Let's change that."

The key slid in smoothly, as if waiting all this time. When I turned it, there was a satisfying click, followed by the faint groan of hinges. A hidden compartment swung open in the base of the lectern, revealing a stack of letters bound with a faded red ribbon.

"Please be recipes," Barb muttered.

"Please be the treasure," Hannah countered.

I untied the ribbon. The top letter was addressed to **My dearest R.** The handwriting was delicate, emotional—the same as the one from the locket.

"It's Eleanor," I said quietly. "These are her letters."

Matt's voice softened. "The ones Gary mentioned."

I read aloud:

My dearest Robert—if the world should ever learn of our truth, may it also learn of our hearts. We never sought riches, only freedom. What is hidden beneath the bell shall clear your name, and mine. Keep faith until dawn, my love.

The rest of the words blurred for a moment as my pulse quickened.

"'Hidden beneath the bell,'" I repeated. "That's not symbolic, is it?"

Matt's gaze followed mine upward toward the belfry ladder. "Knowing this town? Probably not."

Barb groaned. "I did not sign up for heights."

I handed her the stack of letters. "You're on preservation duty."

Hannah and I climbed first, Sadie barking encouragement below. The air grew colder the higher we went, and by the time we reached the small landing, the sunrise had turned the stained glass below into a pool of molten gold.

The bell loomed above us, dark bronze and massive. Dust coated the beam like a fine layer of history.

"'Beneath the bell,'" I said, crouching. The wooden platform beneath had a small hatch secured with a simple latch. I tugged it open, revealing a narrow cavity lined with old cloth. Inside rested a small metal box—different from the others. Polished silver, with a heart engraved on top.

Hannah whistled softly. "That's it. The jackpot."

I lifted it carefully and carried it down the ladder, my heart pounding.

Matt took it from me once my feet hit solid ground. He examined the lid. "No lock this time."

I nodded. "Then let's see what's worth all this trouble."

Inside was a folded legal document, brittle with age, and a single photograph. The picture showed Eleanor and Robert again—but this time, they were standing in front of the town hall, holding hands. At their feet lay a small metal case identical to the one in Matt's hand.

The document was a deed transfer. **Willow Creek Farm**, hereby bequeathed to **Robert Ramsey**, held in trust until such time as the debts of **Reginald Wexler** are cleared. Signed, **Eleanor Wexler**.

"Willow Creek Farm," I said, stunned. "She gave it to him."

Matt's brow furrowed. "So the treasure isn't gold. It's land."

"Land and the right to reclaim it," Barb said. "If the deed was never filed, it's still hidden property."

Hannah grinned. "So the fortune might still be out there. Under Hemlock's herbs and creepy greenhouse vibes!"

Matt gave her a look. "Let's not jump to conclusions."

I smiled faintly. "Jumping to conclusions is kind of our brand."

Sadie barked once, as if to punctuate the statement.

Matt tucked the deed and photo into a folder. "We'll have to check county records. If this was never transferred, the paper trail might lead to who buried it—and why someone wants it uncovered now."

"And whoever's leaving these clues," I added. "They're not done."

As we stepped outside, the sun finally broke over the horizon, flooding the cemetery in gold. The mist burned away, leaving the angel statues gleaming like they'd been freshly polished.

Hannah tilted her face toward the light. "So... what now?"

I looked toward the distant shape of Willow Creek Farm, half hidden by trees. "Now," I said, "we pay Mr. Hemlock another visit."

Sadie barked twice, trotting ahead toward the car.

Barb sighed. "At least tell me we're stopping for more muffins first."

"Of course," I said, smiling. "Even detectives need breakfast."

But as we walked back down the hill, the wind picked up again, carrying the faintest sound of a bell tolling behind us. Once, twice, three times.

When I turned, the chapel door stood ajar.

And I could've sworn, just for a moment, that the angel over Eleanor Wexler's grave was smiling.

Chapter 8

Troubles Among the Nutmegs

By the time we reached Willow Creek Farm again, the mist had burned away, leaving the kind of sunlight that looks pretty in pictures but lies about the temperature. The fields shimmered gold and brittle, the old barn casting a long shadow across the gravel drive.

Sadie barked once as if to announce our arrival—or possibly to warn the local wildlife that the investigation team was back.

Hannah clutched the folded deed like it might bite her. "So, just to clarify," she said, "we're confronting an eccentric spice farmer who may or may not be sitting on the missing Wexler fortune?"

"Exactly," I said. "And doing it before lunch, which should earn us some sort of hazard pay."

Barb, who had volunteered herself again with the promise of "moral support and baked goods," snorted. "I brought cinnamon scones. That's as much morale as I've got."

Matt parked his cruiser behind my Mini Cooper and stepped out, his expression grim but steady. "Let's keep this friendly," he said. "We don't have a warrant, and Hemlock doesn't owe us answers."

Hannah muttered, "He owes us nutmeg at the very least."

Sadie sneezed in apparent agreement.

The farmhouse door opened before we could knock. Hemlock stood there, the morning light catching in his pale eyes. He looked more weathered than he had the day before, like the years had added a few extra just overnight.

"Back so soon," he said, voice dry as kindling. "Didn't expect the law and his entourage."

"Good morning to you, too," I said cheerfully. "We were hoping to ask a few more questions about the farm."

"I figured as much," he replied, stepping aside. "You're not the first to come looking for ghosts, Miss Fisher. But you might be the first to find one."

That earned him a collective pause. Even Matt's jaw twitched.

Inside, the farmhouse smelled like old wood, coffee, and something earthy—herbs, maybe, or secrets steeping too long.

Jars lined every surface, and the floorboards creaked like they were keeping time with our heartbeats.

I glanced at the kitchen table. A single cup of tea sat waiting, steam curling upward.

"Expecting company?" I asked.

"Always do," Hemlock said. He gestured for us to sit. "You said Teresa once came here for nutmeg."

"That's right," I said, watching him carefully. "And we found a deed she signed over to Robert Ramsey. For this property."

His expression didn't change, but the temperature in the room did.

"That's not possible," he said flatly.

Hannah produced the document and set it on the table. "This says otherwise."

Hemlock adjusted his glasses and leaned forward, the paper trembling faintly beneath his fingers. For a long time, no one spoke. Then, finally, he said, "I've seen this handwriting before. My father worked for the Wexlers. He told me Ramsey was cheated out of what was his. That they buried the evidence right here when the family imploded."

"Then you believe it's real?" Matt asked.

Hemlock hesitated. "I believe this land has been fought over since before I was born. Ramsey tried to claim it, but the county clerk's records disappeared that same year. When the Wexlers fell, so did the proof."

Barb crossed her arms. "Convenient timing."

He gave a humorless smile. "Marigold Lake runs on convenient timing."

I took a breath. "Mr. Hemlock... do you know if there's anything still here? Something the Wexlers hid?"

His gaze slid to the window overlooking the greenhouse. "Depends what you mean by here. The farm's old bones go deep. Some say Ramsey planted a safe under the herb beds."

"A buried safe," Hannah breathed. "Now we're talking treasure!"

"Or a hundred pounds of fertilizer," Barb muttered. "Knowing our luck."

Matt looked at Hemlock. "Would you object if we had a look?"

Hemlock's expression turned contemplative. "You'll find what you find. But don't expect it to like being found."

It wasn't the answer I wanted, but it was permission enough.

We stepped out into the greenhouse. The scent hit me first—warm earth, citrus peel, and something faintly metallic. The glass panes glimmered with condensation, turning the sunlight into watery gold.

Sadie darted down the narrow aisle between the tables, her nose working overtime.

Hannah trailed behind her, muttering like a tour guide. "And here we see the rare and deadly *Nutmeg of Doom.* Please do not feed the specimens."

"Keep it up," Barb said, "and I'm selling tickets."

I crouched near the far corner where a patch of thyme had given way to bare soil. The ground there looked different—darker, looser. "Matt," I said, pointing. "Looks like it's been disturbed."

He joined me, squatting to examine the spot. "Could be animals," he said, though his tone suggested he didn't buy it.

Sadie barked once, sharp and certain. Then she began digging.

"Or it could be Sadie," I said.

Within moments, her little paws struck something solid. A hollow clunk echoed beneath the soil.

Matt grabbed a nearby spade, and together we cleared away the dirt until a small metal box emerged—rectangular, heavy, its hinges rusted.

"Well, I'll be," Barb said softly. "That's not fertilizer."

Hannah crouched beside it, her eyes wide. "This is it. This is totally it."

I brushed dirt from the lid. The same heart symbol was etched into the metal, faint but visible. My pulse quickened. "Help me lift it."

It took both Matt and me to haul it onto the table. The lid resisted but finally gave way with a screech. Inside, wrapped in oilcloth, were stacks of paper—ledgers, receipts, and what looked like old correspondence.

"Accounting records," Matt said, flipping through the top layer. "Wexler Lumber Company."

"Anything about the missing money?" I asked.

He scanned a few pages, then stopped. "Maybe." He held one up. "These aren't standard entries. They're coded—see these initials?"

"RR," I read. "Robert Ramsey."

Hannah peered over his shoulder. "So the love interest was keeping the books?"

"Or hiding the evidence," Matt said. "These ledgers could prove the embezzlement wasn't his doing."

I looked down at the papers, the faded ink, the scrawl that had outlasted everyone who wrote it. The realization hit like a slow-moving wave. "Eleanor buried these to protect him. That's what she meant by clearing his name."

Barb whistled. "Decades of gossip undone by good filing habits."

Sadie sneezed, unimpressed.

I turned to Hemlock, who stood in the doorway, arms folded. "Did you know this was here?"

He shook his head. "I knew there were secrets in this soil. I just didn't know whose."

Matt slid one of the ledgers into an evidence sleeve. "We'll need to get these preserved. If this matches with county records, it could reopen the case."

Hannah blinked. "Wait—there's still a case?"

Matt gave her a look. "When there's money missing and people sabotaging trucks, yes."

That sobered her.

I glanced at the door. "So... what now?"

Matt answered before anyone else could. "Now we find out who's been leaving you those clues. Because whoever's doing it wanted you to find this."

Barb tilted her head. "Maybe they wanted her to find it for them."

The thought sank in like a stone. "And now they know we have it."

As if on cue, the wind shifted outside, rattling the greenhouse panels. The sound was high and sharp, like something scraping against glass. Sadie's ears perked up. She barked, staring toward the back wall.

Matt moved first, flashlight out. "Stay here."

He pushed open the back door, disappearing into the tall grass.

A few tense seconds later, his voice called, "Footprints. Fresh ones. Somebody was watching."

Barb muttered a few words not fit for Sunday service.

Hannah clutched Sadie's leash tighter. "What do we do now?"

I took a steadying breath. "We finish what we started."

Matt returned, his expression grim. "Whoever it was knew the land. They're gone now." He nodded at the box. "We'll take this to the station, lock it up. I'll have the documents copied."

Hemlock's gaze flicked to the box, then back to me. "If you stir the past too hard, it tends to boil over."

"Maybe," I said. "But some things need to come to a boil before they can settle."

That earned a faint smile from him, weary but approving.

As we carried the box toward the car, I felt the weight of it through the handle—a century of greed and guilt condensed into thirty pounds of paper.

Hannah opened the passenger door and helped Sadie jump inside. Barb slid into the back seat, muttering something about "coffee stronger than the plot."

Before I got in, I glanced back toward the farmhouse. Hemlock stood on the porch, watching us. Behind him, the greenhouse gleamed in the sunlight, the panes flashing like mirrors.

Something about the scene felt final, and yet not.

"Claire," Matt said quietly, "you okay?"

"Yeah," I said, though it wasn't entirely true. "It's just... every answer feels like another door."

He nodded. "Welcome to investigation."

As we pulled onto the road, the farmhouse disappeared behind a curve. The box sat between us, heavy and silent. Sadie rested her head on my armrest, eyes half-closed, content in her own brand of calm.

But when we passed the edge of the Hemlock property, she suddenly lifted her head and barked once—low, alert.

"What is it, girl?" Hannah asked.

Sadie turned to the window, ears pricked.

For just a second, I thought I saw a figure standing at the tree line—a flash of dark coat, a glint of sunlight on metal. Then it was gone.

Matt must have seen it too, because his hands tightened on the wheel. "We're not done," he said.

"No," I agreed softly. "We're just getting to the heart of it."

And somewhere behind us, hidden among the nutmeg and thyme, the wind whispered through the greenhouse panes—like laughter, or warning.

Chapter 9

Ledgers and Loose Ends

By the time we reached the police station, the box of ledgers had developed its own gravitational pull. Every time I looked at it, my stomach twisted like it knew we'd just changed something that couldn't be undone.

Marigold Lake's police department sat wedged between the library and Murphy's Bakery—proof that the town prioritized carbs and gossip in equal measure. Inside, the air smelled faintly of burnt coffee and copy toner.

Matt carried the box into his office, setting it gently on his desk. "All right," he said. "Let's see what's worth decades of secrets."

Hannah leaned over the edge of the desk, wide-eyed. "It's like opening Pandora's filing cabinet."

Barb plopped into a chair. "Hopefully this time hope isn't the last thing in the box."

Sadie hopped onto the visitor's chair beside me, her tail nub tapping a steady rhythm against the cushion.

Matt began unpacking the ledgers, stacking them carefully. Each was labeled with a year—1962 through 1965—and bound with yellowed string. The last one bore the faint initials **R.R.** burned into the leather.

He pulled on gloves before opening the top ledger. "If these are genuine, they could show where the Wexler money went."

I leaned closer, scanning the faded ink. The pages were filled with neat, deliberate handwriting—columns of numbers, initials, and occasional notes in the margins.

"What's that symbol?" Hannah asked, pointing to a small heart drawn beside several entries.

Matt frowned. "I don't know. It's not part of standard bookkeeping."

Barb tilted her head. "Could be Eleanor's mark. You said she hid things for Ramsey, right?"

"Maybe she marked which accounts were tied to him," I said. "Like a secret code between them."

Matt flipped a few more pages, then paused. "Here. Look at this."

The entry read:

Deposit: Willow Creek Holdings – Transfer of prop-

erty. Payment received: $15,000. Not recorded through Wexler accounts.

"Willow Creek Holdings," I repeated. "That's the farm."

"And fifteen thousand dollars in 1963 money," Barb said, whistling softly. "That's not exactly chump change."

Matt nodded. "If Ramsey transferred money out of Wexler's books under a fake company name, that could be the 'missing fortune.' But the signature on this entry—" He squinted. "—that's Reginald Wexler's handwriting."

"So he knew," I said. "He wasn't robbed. He moved the money himself."

"Or someone forged his name," Matt countered. "Either way, it explains why someone doesn't want these ledgers in daylight."

Hannah frowned. "So the treasure wasn't gold coins or diamonds—it was stolen money disguised as business transfers?"

"Looks that way," Matt said. "And if the land was deeded to Ramsey, that was his insurance policy. Wexler hid money in the farm, Ramsey got the property. Eleanor probably tried to protect them both."

I sank into the chair opposite his desk. "And now someone's trying to finish what they started."

Barb reached for the stack of envelopes on the corner of his desk. "Have you checked the incoming mail lately?"

Matt raised an eyebrow. "No, because I was busy unearthing history with you people."

She rifled through and pulled out a small padded envelope with no return address. "Well, congratulations. History mailed you back."

My stomach dropped. "You're kidding."

"Nope. Postmarked yesterday." She handed it over. "Go on. You're the designated magnet for weird mail."

I tore it open carefully. Inside was a folded piece of paper and a single photograph. The picture showed the four of us—me, Matt, Hannah, and Sadie—standing outside the greenhouse at Willow Creek Farm. It had been taken that morning.

"Oh, that's not creepy at all," Hannah said, her voice going high and thin.

Matt's expression hardened. "They're watching us."

I unfolded the note. Same purple ink, same elegant script:

You've opened doors that should have stayed shut.

The heart beats once more, but some secrets should stay buried.*

Stop digging, or someone gets hurt.*

There was no signature, but the flourish beneath the last line looked like a looping **W**.

I swallowed hard. "They know we found the ledgers."

Barb's voice was quiet. "Whoever's leaving these clues—they're done playing treasure hunt."

Matt set the note aside, his jaw tight. "I'll get the tech team to check for prints. And I'll have patrols sweep the area around the B&B."

"You think they'd come after me?" I asked.

"I think you've made yourself the centerpiece of someone's obsession," he said. "And I don't like it."

Hannah stood abruptly. "So what do we do? Just sit here and wait for another purple-ink threat to arrive in the mail?"

"No," Matt said. "We get ahead of it." He flipped open another ledger, scanning the last few pages. "These entries stop abruptly mid-October 1965. Same time as the Wexler Waltz. Whatever happened that night froze everything in place."

Barb reached for the ledger marked 1964 and opened it at random. "What about this? There's a notation here—**'Finch Agreement – delivery fulfilled.'**"

My pulse jumped. "Finch. Hemlock mentioned that name—Dandelion Finch, a spice trader who disappeared."

Matt nodded. "If Finch handled spice imports, he could've smuggled more than nutmeg. Money, documents, anything that needed to vanish quietly."

"So Finch was the courier," I said. "He helped Wexler move the money, then disappeared when the deal went bad."

"And whoever's leaving the clues wants the rest of it," Barb added.

Matt rubbed his temple. "We'll cross-check any surviving import manifests. But Finch is probably long dead."

"Maybe," I said softly. "But somebody knows what he did."

Sadie let out a low whine, resting her chin on my knee. The office felt suddenly smaller, the air thicker.

Matt closed the ledger and sat back. "Claire, I need you to promise me you'll stay at the Morning Glory tonight. Doors locked, phone on, no midnight strolls."

"Define stroll," I said automatically.

His eyes narrowed. "I'm serious."

I nodded, trying to ignore the weight pressing behind my ribs. "All right. But if someone's trying to scare me off, it's not working. I want to see this through."

Barb grinned faintly. "That's our Claire. Curiosity first, self-preservation somewhere after coffee."

Hannah's phone buzzed, and she frowned at the screen. "Uh... guys? Nanette just texted me. She says someone broke into the Historical Society last night."

Matt straightened. "When last night?"

"Between midnight and two a.m., according to the security camera timestamp. They didn't take money—just old files. Leona's filing a report right now."

"What files?" I asked.

"She didn't say. Just that the Wexler archives are missing."

For a moment, no one spoke. Then Matt swore under his breath. "They're cleaning up the trail."

Barb looked at me. "So much for leaving things buried."

I stood and grabbed my coat. "We need to go to the Historical Society."

"Not 'we,'" Matt said. "Me. You're going home."

I stared at him. "You really think I can sit this out?"

He met my gaze for a long moment, then sighed. "Fine. But you stay in the car."

"Define stay."

"Claire."

I raised a hand. "Fine. I'll stay in the car... mostly."

He didn't believe me, and we both knew it.

We reached the Historical Society within ten minutes. The front door's lock was broken, hanging slightly askew. Inside, light pooled across the floor from a single flickering fluorescent bulb.

Leona Brandt stood near her desk, looking more furious than frightened. "I leave for one night," she snapped, "and some fool decides to redecorate."

Her shelves were in disarray, papers scattered like confetti. One entire filing drawer sat open, empty.

"Which files are missing?" Matt asked.

"The Wexler ones, of course," Leona said bitterly. "And before you ask, no, I don't keep digital backups. This isn't NASA."

I crouched near the desk, scanning the floor. "Whoever did this knew exactly what they were looking for. No wasted effort."

Leona crossed her arms. "They also knew where the key was hidden. Inside the drawer lining. Only a few people knew about that."

I looked up sharply. "Who, exactly?"

She hesitated. "Myself, Nanette—she volunteers here sometimes—and one other person."

"Who?" Matt asked.

Leona's eyes flicked to me, then away. "Your aunt, Teresa."

My stomach flipped. "My aunt?"

"She helped me catalog the Wexler archives twenty years ago. Said she wanted the truth preserved."

Barb let out a low whistle. "Looks like Aunt Teresa's legacy just keeps expanding."

Leona bent to pick up a scattered folder. "She warned me this would happen one day—that the past doesn't stay buried forever. I thought she meant metaphorically."

Sadie sniffed at a pile of torn envelopes near the door and began barking. I walked over, crouched, and froze.

The torn envelopes were stamped **Marigold County Records – Property Transfer Notices.** Every one of them had been ripped open and emptied.

"Someone's tracking the deeds," I said. "They're trying to find every piece of Wexler property."

Matt straightened, face grim. "And they just got a twenty-year head start."

Hannah looked between us. "So what now?"

"Now," I said, "we find out who's still benefiting from Wexler money—and who's willing to kill to protect it."

Outside, the wind picked up, rattling the sign on the door. Sadie pressed against my leg, her tail still but her eyes alert.

Matt met my gaze. "We'll go through what we have at the station. I'll get my team to cross-check the ledgers against current property owners."

I nodded. "And I'll check Teresa's notes back at the B&B. If she worked on these archives, she might've left her own copies."

"Claire—"

"I'll be careful," I said. "Promise."

He exhaled. "You'd better. Because whoever's behind this isn't done yet."

As we stepped outside, dawn light had shifted to late morning, and the town hummed awake around us. Shop windows opened, birds chattered, and somewhere down the street, the church bells began to ring the hour.

The sound should've been comforting. Instead, it felt like a countdown.

Chapter 10

The Memory Keepers Desk

By the time we pulled into the Morning Glory's gravel drive, the scent of cinnamon and coffee drifted through the open windows like an apology from the universe. For a second, I could almost pretend everything was normal—until I remembered the threat letter tucked in Matt's jacket pocket and the fact that someone had been photographing us at Willow Creek Farm.

"Home sweet possibly-bugged home," Hannah said as we climbed out.

"Let's not borrow paranoia," I replied, though I checked the porch anyway. Nothing looked disturbed—same fall wreath, same welcome mat, same faint paw prints from Sadie's last adventure in the flowerbeds.

Barb followed us up the steps, carrying a basket of scones like it was an emotional support animal. "I brought these just in case we have to barricade ourselves in," she said. "They'll go stale before the danger passes, but it's the thought that counts."

Sadie darted ahead, tail nub wagging, and stopped at the front door. She gave one sharp bark.

Matt frowned. "She usually greets, not warns."

I tested the knob. It turned easily. "That's odd. I locked up this morning."

Hannah's grin vanished. "Please tell me you mean metaphorically locked up."

I pushed the door open slowly. The faint chime of the entry bell sounded far too cheerful for the moment. The lobby looked fine—no broken glass, no overturned furniture—but something was off. The air carried the faint metallic tang of dust that's been disturbed.

Matt scanned the room, hand resting lightly on his hip where his badge gleamed. "Stay behind me."

We followed him into the parlor. The curtains were drawn halfway, and one of the cushions on the couch was turned wrong side up. A small detail, but I noticed it instantly—Aunt Teresa's sense of symmetry was practically a religion.

"In here," Barb whispered, pointing toward the back hallway. "Your office light's on."

I hadn't left it on.

Matt pushed the door open with his shoulder. The office looked like a paper tornado had passed through—drawers open, folders scattered, the file cabinet half-emptied. Aunt Teresa's old roll-top desk stood in the corner, the top locked but the key still in the slot. Whoever had been here hadn't bothered to be subtle.

I moved toward it slowly, heart thudding. "This is where she kept her notes. Her journals, old receipts, ledgers—everything."

Hannah crouched beside a pile of loose papers. "They were looking for something specific. See how they left most of this?" She held up a guest ledger from 2008. "Not exactly high-stakes material."

Barb scanned the room, jaw tight. "No signs of forced entry. Whoever it was either had a key or knew how to pick one."

Matt nodded grimly. "We'll dust for prints, but don't expect miracles. If they got into the Historical Society without leaving evidence, they're careful."

Sadie sniffed along the baseboards, nose twitching. She stopped suddenly, pawing at the rug near the desk.

I knelt beside her and pulled the rug back. Beneath it, a small panel was set into the hardwood—one I'd never noticed. "Well, would you look at that," I murmured.

Barb leaned in. "Secret compartments. Why do the bad guys always miss the obvious ones?"

The panel lifted easily, revealing a shallow space lined with cedar. Inside lay a slim leather-bound notebook and a folded piece of paper tied with a faded green ribbon.

Hannah gasped softly. "Is that Aunt Teresa's handwriting?"

It was. Even after all these years, I'd know those looping letters anywhere.

I untied the ribbon and unfolded the paper. It was a list—columns of names, dates, and property titles. At the top, written in her neat script, were the words: **Wexler Holdings – Revised Record, copied from originals before transfer to archives, 2003.**

"She made her own copy," I said, voice barely above a whisper.

Matt crouched beside me. "And hid it under the floor. Smart woman."

Barb frowned. "Why would she copy the records if she trusted the Historical Society?"

"Maybe she didn't," I said. "Or maybe she knew someone else would come for them one day."

Hannah peered over my shoulder. "There are more names here than we've seen before. Look—half these properties still exist. Marigold Hardware, the mill, even Murphy's Bakery."

Matt's eyes narrowed. "If these were part of Wexler assets, that means several current business owners are sitting on old money without realizing it."

"Or realizing it very well," Barb said dryly. "Murphy didn't get that new mixer on tips alone."

I traced my finger down the list until one name jumped out at me—**Finch Import Company**, still listed as active. "That's the same name from the ledgers. Dandelion Finch. And it's listed under an address right here in town."

Matt checked his phone. "That's on Hawthorne Street. Industrial district. The building's been vacant for years."

Hannah's grin returned, despite herself. "Vacant buildings are where all the good mysteries happen."

"Vacant buildings are also where people get murdered," Barb muttered.

Sadie sneezed, unimpressed by either argument.

Matt looked at me. "You're not going there alone."

"I wasn't planning to," I said, though we both knew *planning* was a flexible term.

He sighed, rubbing his temple. "I'll get a warrant and a backup unit. We'll go in daylight. Promise me you'll stay put until then."

"I'll try," I said.

"Claire."

"I'll try really hard."

He gave me that look—the one that managed to mix fondness and exasperation in equal measure—then turned to leave. "I'll be back within the hour. Lock the doors behind me."

After he left, the house felt oddly still. The kind of quiet that doesn't comfort—it listens.

Hannah set Sadie's water bowl down with a sigh. "Do you think whoever broke in found anything?"

"If they had," I said, glancing at the still-locked roll-top desk, "they wouldn't have left in such a hurry."

Barb sat in the armchair by the window, crossing her legs. "What's in the desk?"

"Teresa's personal journal," I said. "She wrote in it every day. Recipes, gossip, town history... and, apparently, cover-ups."

Hannah eyed me. "You're going to open it, aren't you?"

"Absolutely," I said, turning the key.

The desk creaked as it rolled open, releasing a faint puff of dust and lavender—the scent Aunt Teresa had used to line the drawers. Inside, everything was meticulously organized. Pens in one holder, stationery in another, and three stacked notebooks tied with colored ribbons.

The top one was labeled simply **Memories – 2003.**

I flipped it open. Her handwriting filled the page in careful lines:

If anyone ever finds this, I hope it's someone with sense and kindness. The Wexler story is not a tale of fortune but of fear.

The money was never the prize—it was leverage. And someone still holds it.

A chill prickled down my spine.

Barb leaned over my shoulder. "Leverage for what?"

I turned the page. The next entry read:

Reginald's money bought silence, but silence can't last forever. The descendants still live among us. They hide behind new names, but blood remembers. If they ever come for what's left, tell Claire to trust her instincts.

"Tell Claire," I whispered.

Hannah gasped. "She knew this would happen."

Before I could respond, Sadie barked sharply. Once. Twice. Then a third time, low and warning.

Barb rose instantly. "What is it, girl?"

Sadie's ears pricked toward the window. I crossed the room and peered through the curtains. A dark sedan sat parked at the far end of the street, engine running. I couldn't see the driver through the glare of the windshield.

Hannah's voice dropped. "Please tell me that's Matt."

"It's not," I said.

The car idled for another beat, then pulled slowly away, turning the corner.

Barb exhaled shakily. "Maybe they were lost."

"Or watching," I said softly.

Matt returned fifteen minutes later, siren-less but urgent. "I just got a call," he said, stepping inside. "Leona Brandt's house was broken into."

My stomach sank. "Leona? Is she—"

"She's fine," he said. "They trashed her study, though. Took her personal journals and anything Wexler-related. Same M.O. as here."

Barb shook her head. "Whoever this is, they're cleaning up history one house at a time."

"Or trying to erase it altogether," Hannah said.

Matt looked at the notebook in my hands. "Anything useful?"

I handed it to him. "Teresa mentions descendants still in town. Hiding under new names."

He flipped a few pages, scanning quickly. "If that's true, our list of suspects just grew exponentially."

"And the clue about 'the heart beating once more'?" I said. "Maybe it means the Wexler bloodline. Someone who wants to reclaim what's theirs."

"Or protect what's left," Matt said.

Sadie whined softly, pressing against my leg. I reached down to stroke her head. "Either way, they're close. Too close."

Barb stood. "Then we don't sleep tonight. We guard the house in shifts. I'll take first watch with a scone and a flashlight."

Hannah groaned. "I'll make coffee."

Matt half-smiled. "You three are a terrible idea and my favorite disaster."

But as he turned to check the lock again, the front bell jingled.

We froze.

No one had approached. The porch was empty. The bell swayed on its hook, ringing softly in the still air.

On the doormat lay another envelope—ivory, unmarked, sealed with a purple wax **W**.

Matt picked it up carefully, gloved this time. "Delivered by hand," he murmured. "Seconds ago."

The wax cracked as he opened it. Inside, a single card bore six words in that same looping script:

You found the heart. Now find mine.

For a moment, no one spoke.

Then Hannah said, very quietly, "Okay, that's the creepiest Valentine ever."

Matt folded the card. "They're escalating. This isn't about history anymore. It's personal."

I met his eyes. "Then it's time we stop reacting and start leading."

He nodded slowly. "Agreed. But whoever wrote this—they're closer than you think."

Sadie growled low, eyes fixed on the front window. Outside, the street was empty. The only sound was the soft rustle of leaves and the faint creak of the sign swinging above the porch.

And for the first time since this treasure hunt began, I wasn't sure who was hunting whom.

Chapter 11

The House that Finch Forgot

By MIDMORNING, THE CLOUDS had rolled in, hanging low and heavy over Marigold Lake like a warning someone forgot to deliver in writing. Even the ducks looked nervous.

Matt parked his cruiser two blocks from the industrial district, just far enough that our little team didn't look like a parade. The Finch Import Company sat at the end of Hawthorne Street, wedged between a shuttered warehouse and a bait shop that had long ago run out of both bait and charm.

The building itself looked exhausted. Its brick façade was cracked and ivy-choked, and the faded sign above the door—**FINCH IMPORTS**—was missing the letter **C**. So technically, it read **FIN H IMPORTS**, which somehow felt fitting.

"Subtle," Barb murmured, peering out the car window. "Nothing screams 'century-old conspiracy' like a building that could double as a set from a post-apocalyptic film."

"Could be worse," Hannah said. "Could say *ITCH IMPORTS.*"

I gave her a look. "Please don't manifest that."

Sadie sat in the backseat, head tilted as she watched a stray leaf blow across the cracked pavement. Her nub tail wagged once. She'd been unusually quiet all morning, as if she sensed the shift in mood.

Matt got out first, scanning the perimeter. "Place looks abandoned," he said. "No signs of recent entry. But the padlock on the side door's new."

"Maybe someone's still using it," I said. "For storage, or to hide something."

Barb pulled a flashlight from her oversized purse. "Either way, we're getting our daily steps in."

We followed Matt around to the side door. The new padlock gleamed like a sore thumb against the rusted metal. He crouched, inspecting it. "Cheap model. Probably bought at Murphy's Hardware."

"Guess we know where the Wexler fortune didn't go," Hannah muttered.

Matt used a small tool to pop the lock open in under ten seconds.

Hannah blinked. "That was both impressive and concerning."

"Occupational hazard," he said, pushing the door open.

The interior smelled of dust, old coffee, and sea salt. Shafts of light filtered through the high windows, illuminating a maze of wooden crates, file cabinets, and long-abandoned shipping equipment. Each crate bore the faded stencil of **Finch Import Company – Marigold Lake, IA.**

"This is incredible," I whispered, stepping inside. "It's like time stopped."

Barb ran her finger along a crate lid, then showed me the layer of dust it left behind. "Time stopped about forty years ago, give or take a sneeze."

Hannah, camera phone in hand, started filming. "This is so going on my feed. #UrbanExplorationMarigoldEdition."

"Post that and I'm confiscating your phone," Matt said without looking up.

She made a face but tucked the phone away. "Fine, no free publicity for our near-death experience."

Sadie trotted ahead, nose twitching, then stopped near a cluster of file cabinets. She barked once, short and sharp.

I followed her and tugged at the drawer she was pawing. It opened with a groan. Inside were dozens of shipping manifests, all stamped with the same name: **R. Ramsey.**

"Robert Ramsey again," I said softly. "This must have been his cover operation."

Matt examined one of the papers. "These shipments came from all over—India, Zanzibar, Ceylon. Nutmeg, cloves, cinnamon..." He trailed off. "And unlisted parcels."

"Unlisted as in illegal?" Barb asked.

"Or unrecorded," he said. "Whatever Finch was doing, he wasn't running a normal import business."

I flipped through a stack of files until something caught my eye—a ledger marked **Personal Correspondence – 1965.** Inside were letters between Finch and Eleanor Wexler.

I read aloud: "*My dear Eleanor, the ledger you requested is complete. The funds are secured beneath the stage as instructed. Should you wish to dissolve our arrangement, you need only destroy the second key.*"

"The stage," I murmured. "The Wexler Waltz. That's where we found the tin."

Hannah's eyes widened. "So Finch helped her hide the ledgers, then vanished."

"Looks like it," I said. "But why resurface now?"

A noise answered for us—a soft metallic clatter somewhere in the shadows near the back of the warehouse.

Matt froze. "Stay here."

"Right," Barb whispered. "Because that always works."

He moved toward the sound, hand hovering near his belt. The rest of us exchanged a glance, then followed anyway—quietly, or at least as quietly as three women and a Boston Terrier can manage on concrete floors.

The far end of the building opened into a narrow corridor lined with shelves of dusty spice tins. A faint draft stirred the air.

"Probably just the wind," Hannah whispered.

"Or a rat," Barb said. "Either way, I'm not screaming first."

Then a voice spoke from the darkness. "You shouldn't be here."

I jumped, nearly dropping the folder in my hands.

A man stepped out from behind a stack of crates. He was tall, thin, and dressed in work clothes too clean for a place that hadn't been used in decades. His face was shadowed under the brim of his cap, but his eyes gleamed—cold and measured.

"Who are you?" Matt asked, his tone calm but edged.

The man smiled faintly. "Caretaker. Been watching this place for years. Finch left me in charge."

Barb squinted. "Left you in charge fifty years ago?"

"His words," the man said with a shrug. "Some promises outlast the people who make them."

Sadie growled low, her stance rigid.

I held up the folder. "If you're the caretaker, maybe you can explain why someone's breaking into homes and stealing Wexler files."

His smile vanished. "People should stop digging up the past."

"That's funny," I said. "We've heard that before. Usually right before someone tries to make us regret it."

Matt stepped forward. "You're connected to the Wexlers."

"Maybe," the man said. "Or maybe I'm just trying to keep their ghosts quiet."

He moved closer, and the light from the window hit his face fully. He was older than I'd guessed—late sixties, maybe seventies—but wiry and sharp, like a blade that refused to dull.

"The name's Daniel Finch," he said. "Dandelion was my father. He started this mess. I'm just trying to end it."

Hannah gasped. "You're that Finch?"

He nodded. "The last one. My father helped the Wexlers move their money out of town when the scandal broke. It was supposed to be temporary—just until things settled. But when Reginald vanished, everything went sideways. The treasure? It's not gold. It's the ledger—the one that proves who took what."

Matt frowned. "We already found ledgers."

"Not that one," Finch said. "The master ledger. It ties the Wexlers' fortune to half the businesses still running in Marigold Lake. If it comes out, the town will tear itself apart."

I crossed my arms. "And you're trying to keep it buried."

"I'm trying to keep the peace," he said. "Some truths do more harm than good."

Barb snorted. "That's the kind of line villains use right before they get caught."

Finch's eyes flicked toward me. "You're Teresa's niece. You're the reason this started again."

My pulse quickened. "What do you mean?"

"She wrote to me before she died," he said. "Said the past was waking up and that she couldn't stop it alone. When I came back to town, the clues had already started circulating. Someone else got to them first."

"Who?" Matt asked.

Finch hesitated. "A woman. Younger. Said she was researching the Wexler legacy. I thought she was a historian. Then files started disappearing, and I realized she wasn't preserving history—she was rewriting it."

I exchanged a glance with Hannah. "Leona Brandt?"

Finch shook his head. "No. Someone else. She called herself **Grace Holloway.**"

The name hit me like a jolt. "Grace Holloway? She ran the Chamber of Commerce years ago."

"She's a Wexler," Finch said flatly. "Changed her name after the scandal. She wants what's left of the fortune—and she doesn't care who gets hurt finding it."

Matt's jaw clenched. "Where is she now?"

Finch shook his head. "If I knew, I'd have stopped her. All I can tell you is this: she's looking for the same ledger you are. And she's closer than you think."

Before we could respond, a sudden crash echoed from the front of the building. Finch spun toward the sound.

"Back!" Matt ordered, moving forward.

The crash was followed by the splintering of wood and the squeal of metal. A dark figure darted through the main doorway, grabbed something from a nearby crate, and vanished into the daylight before any of us could react.

When we reached the door, the street was empty except for a single tire mark curving away toward the lake.

"They took something," Finch said, breathing hard. He pointed to the crate. The lid was open, and inside was an empty space where a small metal box had been.

Matt cursed under his breath. "What was in there?"

"The master ledger," Finch said grimly. "It's gone."

For a moment, no one spoke. The air felt heavier than before, thick with dust and defeat.

Barb broke the silence. "Well, this has officially gone from cozy to chaos."

Finch turned to me, his eyes sharp again. "You need to end this, Claire. Before she does."

"And how exactly do you suggest I do that?" I asked.

He looked at Sadie, then back at me. "The last clue isn't written down. It's hidden where Teresa kept her most precious memories."

"The B&B," I whispered.

He nodded once. "You'll find what she wanted you to see. But hurry. If Grace Holloway has the ledger, she's already halfway there."

Matt exhaled, rubbing the back of his neck. "This keeps getting better."

Barb patted his arm. "Cheer up. At least we have snacks."

But I barely heard them. My mind was already spinning, fitting puzzle pieces together like a picture coming into focus.

Aunt Teresa's notes. The Wexlers' secrets. Grace Holloway. It all pointed back to the same place—home.

As we stepped out into the gray morning, Sadie trotted ahead toward the car, tail wagging with cautious excitement.

"Back to the Morning Glory?" Hannah asked.

"Back to the heart of it," I said.

Because if Aunt Teresa had hidden the truth in her home, it meant one thing: the final secret of the Wexlers—and whoever was willing to kill for it—had been waiting under my roof the whole time.

Chapter 12

Shadows in the Hall

THE DRIVE BACK TO the Morning Glory felt longer than usual, even though the streets of Marigold Lake were mostly empty. The clouds hung so low they looked like they might bump the church steeple.

Hannah was in the passenger seat scrolling frantically through her phone, muttering, "Grace Holloway, Grace Holloway..." under her breath. Barb sat in the back with Sadie in her lap, stroking her ears absently. Sadie, ever perceptive, was unusually still.

"Anything?" I asked.

Hannah shook her head. "She's a ghost online. There's a LinkedIn from like 2012 for a *Grace H. Holloway – Historical Preservation Consultant*, but no recent posts, no social media, no current address."

"People who steal ledgers and rewrite history don't usually keep up with their Instagram reels," Barb said dryly.

Matt's cruiser led the way up the hill toward the B&B. He signaled us to park behind him, then walked over to my window. "You three stay in the car until I've checked inside."

"Define 'stay,'" I started, but he gave me that look—the one that meant don't push it.

So I didn't. Out loud.

We watched him disappear through the front door, one hand resting on his holster. The seconds stretched long enough for Hannah to start bouncing her leg.

After two full minutes, he reappeared and waved us forward.

Inside, everything looked... normal. Too normal. The air was thick with the scent of cinnamon from the morning scones, and sunlight filtered lazily through the lace curtains. But there was a weight in the room—the kind that comes from knowing someone else might have touched your things.

"No new damage," Matt said. "Doors still locked. Windows intact. Whoever broke in earlier hasn't been back."

"That we know of," Barb murmured.

I moved toward Aunt Teresa's desk, now closed and locked again, the key resting where I'd left it. "If Finch was right, what we're looking for is hidden where she kept her most precious memories."

"That could be anywhere," Hannah said. "Photo albums? Her recipe box? Maybe the diary you found?"

I opened the roll-top desk again. The scent of lavender met me like an old friend. "She wrote everything down. There has to be a clue."

Matt crouched beside the desk, checking the baseboards. "Nothing obvious. Maybe a false back?"

Barb tapped her chin. "If I were hiding a secret, I'd put it somewhere sentimental. Teresa was practical, but she loved her symbols. You said she called herself the Keeper of Memories."

"Right," I said. "So maybe the clue isn't in her desk—it's near something tied to memories."

Sadie barked once and trotted toward the hallway leading to the guest rooms.

"Or maybe," Barb said, standing, "we follow the dog."

We trailed Sadie down the hall. She stopped in front of the shadow box on the wall—Aunt Teresa's Memory Frame. It was filled with trinkets from decades of Morning Glory history: old room keys, a pressed marigold, a postcard from the inn's grand opening, a photograph of Teresa and a much younger Matt standing beside the old sheriff.

Sadie pawed at the bottom corner.

Hannah leaned closer. "That photo—wait, that's the old town hall in the background. The Wexler Waltz night."

I peered closer. The photo's date was scrawled on the back of the frame: **October 14, 1965.** The same week the ledgers stopped.

Matt frowned. "This wasn't here last month."

"No," I said slowly. "It wasn't."

I lifted the frame off the wall. It was heavier than I expected. On the back, beneath the paper backing, something crinkled. I tore the edge carefully and found a folded envelope taped to the wood.

The paper was yellowed but sealed with the same wax **W** we'd seen before.

Hannah held her breath. "Please tell me this isn't another threatening Valentine."

I cracked the seal. Inside was a single piece of paper, the ink faded but still legible in Aunt Teresa's familiar hand:

For whoever carries on my search—look beneath the heart that beats without blood. There you'll find the truth I couldn't speak.

Barb raised an eyebrow. "The heart that beats without blood. That's either poetic or horrifying."

Matt looked thoughtful. "A clock. A pendulum."

I turned toward the parlor. "The grandfather clock."

The clock had stood by the front window since before I was born—oak, ornate, with a carved heart motif above the face. Aunt Teresa called it her "heartbeat of the house."

I knelt beside it, running my fingers along the carved edge until I felt a small indentation near the base. With a soft click, a hidden panel slid open.

Inside was a wooden box, no bigger than a loaf of bread, wrapped in lace and tied with a faded blue ribbon.

"Bingo," Barb whispered.

I pulled it out and set it on the coffee table. My hands trembled slightly as I untied the ribbon. Inside were stacks of letters, bound together with twine, and a small velvet pouch.

Hannah leaned over my shoulder. "Please let that be jewels."

I opened the pouch. Inside was not jewelry but a key—old, brass, and shaped like a heart.

Another heart.

Matt examined it. "Same design as the one from the chapel, but older. Heavier."

I unfolded the top letter.

My dearest sister, it began, in Aunt Teresa's looping script. *If you are reading this, then I have failed to stop the past from repeating. The woman who calls herself Grace Holloway is not what she seems. She seeks not treasure, but control. The master ledger was divided long ago, its pages scattered to protect the innocent. But the last piece—my piece—remains here at the Morning Glory. It must never fall into the wrong hands.*

I felt my throat tighten. "She knew. She knew Grace would come."

Barb frowned. "Then where's the piece she's talking about?"

105

Before anyone could answer, Sadie began barking again—loud, insistent, the kind of bark that says someone's here.

Matt was on his feet instantly, gun drawn. "Stay back."

A floorboard creaked above us.

Hannah's eyes widened. "Please tell me you rent out the attic."

I shook my head. "No one's stayed up there in months."

Another creak. Then the soft sound of footsteps crossing the upper hallway.

Matt signaled for silence, then moved toward the staircase. We followed at a cautious distance, Sadie at my heel, trembling with alertness.

The stairs groaned with every step. At the top, the air smelled faintly of dust and cedar. The door to the attic stood slightly ajar. A sliver of light spilled through the gap.

Matt nudged it open. The attic was cluttered with boxes, old quilts, and forgotten furniture. A single bulb hung from the ceiling, swinging gently.

"Police," Matt said sharply. "Come out."

No answer.

He stepped inside, motioning for us to stay back. Then, from behind a stack of trunks, came a sudden movement—a shadow darting toward the window.

"Stop!"

The figure didn't. The window flew open with a crash, and a gust of cold air rushed in. Matt lunged, grabbing the edge of a sleeve, but the intruder twisted free and dropped onto the porch roof below, then down to the ground with surprising agility.

I ran to the window in time to see a woman sprinting across the yard. She wore dark jeans, a gray jacket, and a scarf that whipped behind her like a flag. Even from that distance, I could make out a streak of silver in her dark hair.

"Grace Holloway," I breathed.

Matt radioed for backup, but by the time he reached the front porch, the woman had vanished into the woods behind the property.

Downstairs, the open box still sat on the coffee table—empty.

Barb pointed. "The key. It's gone."

My stomach dropped. "She took it."

Matt swore softly. "She was here the whole time. Waiting."

Hannah clutched Sadie. "But how did she even get in? We were here the entire morning!"

I closed my eyes, replaying the last few hours. The sedan. The envelope. The bell ringing with no one there.

"She was already inside," I said quietly. "She left the letter to distract us."

Barb exhaled shakily. "Well, it worked."

Matt glanced out the window toward the lake. "We'll track her. She can't get far."

I shook my head. "She doesn't need to. She has the key—and whatever it unlocks."

The air felt heavier, colder. The once-cheerful parlor now looked like a stage after the play ended—props still standing, but the illusion broken.

Hannah rubbed her arms. "What do we do now?"

I looked at the grandfather clock, its pendulum still swinging in steady rhythm. "We do what Teresa wanted—we finish it."

Barb nodded firmly. "And we start with that lake. If I were hiding a final secret, I'd put it somewhere nobody wanted to swim."

Matt holstered his weapon. "We'll regroup. But you're not going anywhere without backup."

"Wouldn't dream of it," I said.

He didn't believe me for a second, and we both knew it.

As he radioed the rest of the department, I glanced again at the letter on the table. Teresa's words echoed in my head: *It must never fall into the wrong hands.*

Outside, the wind shifted, carrying the faint sound of water lapping against the dock. The lake shimmered gray and cold beneath the lowering sky.

Sadie pressed against my leg, eyes wide, as if she felt it too—that the treasure hunt was over, and the reckoning had just begun.

Chapter 13

Beneath the Surface

By the time we reached the lake, the clouds had broken just enough to let streaks of sunlight hit the water like scattered coins. The breeze carried the scent of wet leaves and cold stone—a reminder that autumn at Marigold Lake could be both beautiful and unforgiving.

Matt's cruiser rolled to a stop near the dock. He got out first, scanning the shoreline. "If Grace came this way, she'll head toward the north path. It leads straight to the old boathouse."

I joined him, Sadie trotting at my heel. "That's where Teresa used to store decorations for the summer festivals," I said. "She called it the *Memory Boat*. Said it kept everything that made the town shine."

"Fitting," Barb said, climbing out behind us with a thermos of coffee in hand. "Let's hope the only thing shining today is a clue."

Hannah adjusted her scarf and shivered. "I can't believe we're doing this without backup."

Matt shot her a look. "They're on the way. But the roads are still blocked by the farmers' market detour."

"Only in Marigold Lake would a treasure-hunt chase get delayed by homemade jam," Barb muttered.

We followed the narrow trail that wound along the lake's edge. The water lapped quietly against the rocks, and the sound of ducks squabbling in the distance added an oddly peaceful soundtrack to the tension building in my chest.

The boathouse came into view—a squat wooden structure with peeling white paint and a sign that once read *Marigold Rentals.* The door hung slightly askew, one hinge rusted through.

Sadie barked twice, nose pointed forward.

"She's here," I said.

Matt motioned for silence and approached the door first. The interior was dim, the air thick with the scent of damp wood and gasoline. Dust motes swirled in the weak light filtering through the cracks in the siding.

A single rowboat rested on its side in the middle of the floor. Beneath it, the boards looked newer—replaced recently.

"Something's under there," I whispered.

Matt knelt, shining his flashlight along the seams. "You're right. Fresh nails, different wood grain."

Barb sighed. "Of course the final clue involves manual labor."

He pried the first board loose with a crowbar from a nearby shelf. The sound echoed across the lake, sharp and hollow. Beneath the plank was a narrow compartment lined with tar paper.

And inside it, a small iron chest.

"Another box," Hannah breathed. "I'm sensing a theme."

The heart-shaped lock glinted faintly.

"The key," I said. "Grace's key."

Matt nodded grimly. "If she's been here, she might've already opened it."

He lifted the chest out carefully. It was heavier than it looked, leaving faint black streaks on his gloves.

"Set it on the dock," I said. "Let's see."

We stepped into the sunlight, the lake shimmering around us. Matt eased the lid up—and stopped.

It wasn't locked.

Inside, resting on a piece of faded blue silk, was a thick ledger bound in leather, its edges charred as if it had survived a fire.

"The master ledger," I whispered. "Finch was right."

But beneath it, something else caught my eye—a folded envelope addressed in the same elegant purple ink as the earlier clues.

Matt picked it up, holding it at arm's length as though expecting it to hiss. "Another message."

He handed it to me. The wax seal bore a different imprint this time: not a "W," but a heart split in two.

To the Keeper of Memories—
You've come farther than I expected. What lies within this book could destroy everything your aunt loved. Walk away now, and you'll keep Marigold Lake whole. Open it, and the truth will pull you under.
— G.H.

"Grace Holloway," Hannah said softly. "She's taunting you."

"Or warning me," I said.

Barb crossed her arms. "Oh, please. People who break into houses don't issue polite warnings."

Matt turned a page of the ledger. The writing inside was faint but legible—columns of numbers, names, and transfers that matched the Wexler files. But the final page was different.

It contained a list of family names—Wexler, Ramsey, Holloway—and beneath them, Caldwell.

I blinked. "Wait—Caldwell?"

Barb looked up sharply. "That's Nanette's maiden name."

Matt frowned. "So Nanette's family was part of this too?"

"Or caught in the middle," I said. "Teresa mentioned the descendants still lived among us. She must've meant the Caldwells too."

Before we could process that, Sadie growled low, staring at the treeline behind us.

A twig snapped.

Matt spun, flashlight sweeping the shadows. "Grace?"

No answer.

Then, from the edge of the trees, a figure emerged—Grace Holloway herself. Her hair was windswept, her gray jacket streaked with dirt, but her posture was unyielding.

"I told you to stop," she said, her voice calm and cold. "That book doesn't belong to you."

Matt stepped between us. "You're under investigation, Ms. Holloway. I suggest you come quietly."

She smiled faintly. "You think this is about me? That ledger is poison. You release it, you'll destroy this town."

"People deserve the truth," I said.

"Truth?" She laughed softly. "The truth is that your aunt helped cover up a theft that saved Marigold Lake from ruin. The Wexlers weren't villains—they were desperate. The money rebuilt the town after the flood. Every shop, every school, every roof—you're standing on stolen gold."

The wind picked up, sending ripples across the lake.

"You expect me to believe that?" I asked.

"I expect you to understand," she said. "Some things are better left buried."

Matt shifted slightly. "Step away from the water, Grace."

But she didn't move. Her gaze locked on me. "You're just like Teresa. Always chasing ghosts. She realized too late that revealing the truth would undo everything she built. Don't make her mistake."

Sadie barked sharply, as if sensing the tension cresting.

Grace's expression softened, almost regretful. "I didn't come to fight, Claire. I came to finish what your aunt started."

Then she turned and hurled the ledger into the lake.

"No!" I lunged forward, but Matt caught me. The book hit the water with a hollow splash and sank instantly.

"You can't let it end like that!" I shouted.

Grace stepped backward toward the edge. "It already ended, years ago. You just didn't know it."

And before Matt could stop her, she disappeared into the woods, leaving only footprints in the mud and a silence that felt too final.

We stood there for a long moment, staring at the ripples spreading across the surface of the lake.

Barb broke the silence first. "Well," she said, "that's one way to close a chapter."

Hannah sniffed. "Literally."

Matt ran a hand through his hair. "We'll drag the lake. Maybe we can recover it."

But I shook my head. "No. If she wanted it gone, she made sure it wouldn't come back."

Sadie whined softly and leaned against my leg.

Barb sighed. "So now what? We just pretend none of this happened?"

I stared at the water, where sunlight danced over the ripples like fading embers. "We find another way. Teresa left breadcrumbs everywhere. She wouldn't trust the truth to just one book."

Matt nodded. "Then we start at the beginning. Check every place she mentioned. Every file, every note."

Hannah looked doubtful. "And if Grace comes back?"

"Then she'll find us waiting," I said.

A sudden gust of wind swept across the dock, carrying a shimmer of leaves onto the water. For a heartbeat, something caught the light—a small glint beneath the surface, right where the ledger had sunk.

I knelt, squinting. "Matt... look."

He followed my gaze. Just below the rippling surface, a metal corner gleamed.

"The box," he said. "It's caught on something."

We found an old boat hook along the dock and used it to snag the edge. The chest rose slowly from the water, heavy and dripping, but intact.

When we opened it again, the ledger was still there—soaked but legible.

Barb grinned. "Guess the truth can swim."

Matt exhaled. "Let's get this back to the station before she tries again."

I wrapped the book in my jacket. The wet leather was cold against my arms, but it felt alive—like the heartbeat Teresa had written about.

As we walked back toward the cars, the clouds finally broke apart, spilling sunlight over the lake. The reflections shimmered, and for a moment, I thought I saw another figure standing across the water—tall, still, watching.

But when I blinked, the shore was empty.

Hannah sighed. "So... celebration pancakes when this is over?"

"Make it waffles," Barb said. "We've earned texture."

Matt smiled faintly but kept his gaze on the treeline. "Let's go. The sooner we decode this, the sooner we end it."

I looked back once more at the lake. The ripples had smoothed into glass, the secret once again hidden beneath its surface.

But I knew better now. Secrets didn't stay buried forever—not in Marigold Lake.

And as Sadie trotted ahead, tail wagging, I felt the first spark of hope that maybe—just maybe—we were close to finally keeping Teresa's promise.

Chapter 14

The Blood Beneath the Ink

By the time we reached the station, the ledger had left a trail of water spots from the car to Matt's desk. The room smelled faintly of damp paper and coffee that had been reheated too many times.

Hannah perched on the edge of a chair, clutching a towel around the dripping book like it was a newborn.
"If anyone asks," she said, "I'm just here for emotional support and scone rations."

Barb poured herself a fresh cup of coffee. "Make that two. We're about to dive into a hundred pages of creative accounting."

Matt laid the ledger flat on his desk. The leather cover, once dark, had taken on a mottled gray sheen from the lake water.

He turned the first few pages carefully, spreading them open with paperweights to keep them from curling.

"Still legible," he said.

"Or unlucky, depending on what's in there," I replied.

Sadie sat at my feet, head resting on her paws but eyes fixed on the book like she knew the truth inside it was about to change everything.

The handwriting was the same we'd seen in the other ledgers—tidy, deliberate, and occasionally annotated in the margins by someone else. But toward the back, the ink grew darker, bolder. Emotional, almost frantic.

"Different hand," Matt said, tracing the pen strokes. "This one's not Reginald Wexler's."

"It's Eleanor's," I said. "You can tell by the loops."

Barb squinted. "You can tell by the loops?"

"I used to study her letters for fun," I said. "It's how Teresa taught me to practice patience."

Hannah grinned. "That explains a lot."

Matt smiled faintly, then refocused on the text. "Here. Listen to this."

He read aloud:

To preserve what's left of the Wexler name, I entrust the balance of our accounts to Teresa Caldwell, Keeper of the Morning Glory. Let her use it to mend what we broke, and let no one ever say the Wexlers took more than they gave.

I felt my chest tighten. "Teresa's name. She was part of it."

Barb's eyebrows shot up. "So your aunt didn't just discover the Wexler scandal—she was the cleanup crew."

"She was the one Eleanor trusted," I said softly. "The heart that beat without blood."

Matt turned the page. "There's more. It lists a single remaining account—Marigold Community Fund. Established 1971. Initial deposit: $125,000."

Hannah's mouth fell open. "That's the scholarship fund! The one that pays for local students' tuition every year."

I stared at the ink until it blurred. "Teresa turned the stolen money into something good. She didn't hide it for herself—she gave it back to the town."

Barb whistled softly. "Well, that's one way to launder your conscience."

Matt leaned back in his chair. "That means the treasure's been here all along. Not gold or jewels—education, charity, the foundation that kept this place alive."

Hannah smiled weakly. "A cozy mystery with a moral compass. I can live with that."

But something tugged at me. "There's still one thing missing."

Barb raised an eyebrow. "Aside from a nap?"

"The reason Teresa kept all this from me," I said. "She could've told me. She could've trusted me."

Matt flipped to the final page. "Maybe she did."

The last entry was written in Teresa's unmistakable hand:

If my niece ever takes up this burden, tell her this: our family was never separate from theirs. Blood binds more than it divides. Claire, you are as much a Wexler as you are a Caldwell. Remember that truth when the time comes to choose what to keep—and what to let go.

The words hit like a physical blow.

"I'm—what?" I managed. "That's not possible."

Matt looked at me gently. "You said your aunt never talked much about her parents."

"She said they were ordinary," I said, my voice hollow. "Small-town people. Hard-working, quiet. There's no way—"

Barb set down her coffee cup slowly. "Honey, this is Marigold Lake. Nobody's parents are ordinary."

Hannah's eyes were wide. "So Teresa was a Wexler descendant who took the money, changed her name, and turned it into something good. That makes you—"

"Half of the legacy she tried to bury," I finished quietly.

For a long moment, no one spoke. Even the hum of the fluorescent lights seemed distant.

Matt closed the ledger gently. "You okay?"

I let out a shaky laugh. "Define okay."

Sadie rested her head on my knee, a comforting weight that anchored me back to the moment. "All this time, I've been running a B&B on the ruins of my family's secrets."

"Or rebuilding it on their redemption," Matt said.

Barb nodded. "And doing a better job of it, if you ask me. Nobody leaves here hungry or un-gossiped-about."

That broke the tension enough for me to smile. "Thanks, Barb."

Hannah frowned, tapping her chin. "But if Teresa hid all this, Grace Holloway must've known the truth too. That's why she wanted the ledger—so no one would learn the Wexler line continued."

"She wanted control," I said. "If the town found out, they'd question everything—her position, her influence. She could claim she was preserving history when really, she was protecting herself."

Matt nodded. "We'll issue an alert and get her photo out to nearby counties. If she's still in the area, someone will spot her."

Barb sighed. "And when they do, I hope she's somewhere without lake access."

Hannah leaned forward, elbows on her knees. "So what happens to the ledger now?"

Matt hesitated, glancing at me. "It's evidence—but it's also part of your family's history. I'll file a copy for the record and return the original to you once the case closes."

I nodded slowly. "I think that's what Teresa would want."

Sadie sneezed, which I decided to interpret as agreement.

Barb stood and stretched. "Well, I'm off to make a casserole for stress management. Anyone want in?"

Hannah perked up. "Only if it's the kind with crushed potato chips on top."

They headed out, bickering amiably. The door swung shut behind them, leaving just Matt, Sadie, and me.

He leaned against the edge of the desk. "You know this changes everything."

"I know," I said. "But maybe it also explains everything."

He smiled faintly. "Teresa would be proud."

I looked down at the ledger, tracing the edge of the leather cover. "She kept so much to protect this town. To protect me. Maybe it's time I stop hiding behind her memory and start owning it."

"You already are," he said.

Sadie barked once, as if seconding the motion.

A knock sounded at the door. It opened slowly, and Nanette Caldwell poked her head in, her expression hesitant but determined. "Did I just hear my name involved in scandal again?"

Barb must have called her.

I stood. "Nanette, you should see this."

She stepped inside, adjusting her glasses as Matt opened the ledger for her. She studied the entries for a long moment, her lips moving as she read.

Finally, she exhaled. "So Teresa did it. She finished what Eleanor started."

"You knew?" I asked softly.

"I suspected," she said. "Your aunt had a way of hinting at big things over tea. But she never said enough for me to be sure. I think she wanted you to find it, Claire. When you were ready."

I felt a lump rise in my throat. "I don't know if I was."

Nanette smiled gently. "Then you did it anyway. That's what being a Caldwell—or a Wexler—really means."

The room went quiet again, but it wasn't a heavy silence this time. It felt like something loosening, finally allowed to breathe.

Matt cleared his throat. "We'll keep digging through the records, but this ledger—this story—it belongs to you now."

I closed the book carefully. "Then I guess I have some rewriting to do. And maybe a new breakfast special to name after our family history."

Hannah's voice drifted from the hallway. "Please don't call it *Scandal Scones!*"

Barb chimed in, "Too late—I already trademarked it!"

Matt chuckled, and even Nanette smiled. The heaviness of the day started to lift, replaced by something steadier—hope, maybe, or closure disguised as caffeine.

Outside, the rain had stopped. The air smelled like fresh earth and possibility.

I looked down at Sadie. "What do you think, girl? Time to head home?"

She barked once, bright and decisive.

As we left the station, I carried the ledger close to my chest. The ink inside might have been written by people long gone, but the story it told—of redemption, resilience, and love tangled up with guilt—wasn't finished.

Not yet.

Because in Marigold Lake, history never truly ends. It just waits for someone brave—or stubborn—enough to turn the next page.

Chapter 15

Rumors and Revelations

BARB IGNORED HER. "ANYWAY, people have a right to know. A million dollars, missing ledgers, nutmeg—it's civic history! Besides, it's boosting business. I heard Murphy's Bakery ran out of scones before nine a.m. due to 'treasure-themed touri sm.'"

Nanette, sitting at the corner table with her reading glasses perched on her nose, sighed. "Lord help us, they're turning it into a festival. I just saw a flyer at the post office for something called *Wexler Weekend*."

I groaned. "You're kidding."

"Nope." She held up the flyer. A cartoon magnifying glass hovered over a drawing of Marigold Lake. Below it: *'Treasure, Truth, and Tea at Two!'*

"Unbelievable," I said. "We can't even keep a missing cat private in this town."

Matt appeared in the doorway, looking far too composed for a man who'd spent the last twelve hours fielding calls from journalists. "You're trending on the town forum," he said, setting his coffee on the counter.

I blinked. "We have a town forum?"

Hannah grinned. "Oh yes. And you're under the thread titled *'Lady Detectives of Marigold Lake.'*"

"Please tell me Sadie's getting credit too."

"Top commenter," Hannah said proudly. "Someone posted a photo of her in her argyle sweater with the caption 'our real hero.'"

Sadie, hearing her name, perked up from her spot under the counter, wagging her nub tail in modest agreement.

Matt leaned closer. "You should be careful, Claire. The mayor's office called this morning."

I sighed. "That can't be good."

"They're concerned that all this 'treasure hysteria' is making the town look unstable. Reed's aide said, and I quote, *'Tell Miss Fisher to keep her B&B in the hospitality business, not the excavation business.'*"

Barb gasped dramatically. "Oh, that man's as crooked as a corkscrew! If there's scandal attached to the Wexlers, you can bet the Reeds are knee-deep in it."

Matt's jaw tightened. "That's what I'm starting to think."

"Wait," Hannah said, her eyes lighting up. "You think Mayor Reed's family is connected to the Wexlers?"

Matt hesitated. "I think there's overlap. The Reeds were partners in several of the Wexler business ventures back in the day. If the ledgers prove financial misconduct, it could tarnish the mayor's legacy—and his reelection."

"So he's trying to shut us down," I said.

"More like slow you down," Matt corrected. "You're drawing attention he can't control."

"Good," Barb said. "About time somebody else ran this circus for a change."

Nanette closed her book. "You'd better tread carefully, Claire. Reed's not the kind of man who likes being embarrassed."

"I'm not trying to embarrass him," I said. "I'm just trying to tell the truth."

"Which, in Marigold Lake," Barb said, "is the same thing."

The room fell quiet for a moment. Outside, the wind rustled through the marigolds in the front garden. For the first time all morning, I felt the weight of what we'd uncovered pressing down like a physical thing.

Matt must've sensed it, because his voice softened. "You don't have to handle this alone, you know."

"I know," I said, meaning it.

Hannah broke the tension. "Speaking of not alone, I've been doing some digging of my own. Figuratively. I cross-referenced the old Wexler property deeds with the names in Teresa's journal."

Barb blinked. "And you understood them?"

"Mostly," Hannah said proudly. "One stood out—an estate listed under Reed-Wexler Holdings. It was sold in the nineties to a shell company, but the buyer's signature looks familiar."

"Familiar how?" Matt asked.

She flipped open her notebook, revealing a photocopy. "Recognize the name?"

Matt's eyes narrowed. "Colton Parrish."

Nanette inhaled sharply. "That name again."

"Who is he?" I asked.

Nanette's expression turned grim. "A man who knows too much about both families—and who's made it his life's work to dig up what others buried. He was close to Eleanor Wexler once. Some say too close."

Barb smirked. "I knew this would circle back to romance."

"Not romance," Nanette said. "Obsession."

A chill ran down my spine. "And he's still around?"

"He left town years ago," Nanette said. "But if his name's resurfacing on property records, he's back. And he's watching."

Matt straightened. "That's our next lead. If Parrish is tied to Reed and Wexler, he may be the link between the old scandal and the current treasure hunt."

I nodded slowly. "Then we find him."

Barb raised her coffee cup. "Operation Nutmeg, Phase Two: *Parrish Pursuit.*"

Hannah grinned. "I'm making shirts."

Nanette looked at me. "If you're going to do this, you'll need someone who remembers that time firsthand."

"Who?"

"Colton wasn't the only one close to Eleanor," she said. "There's someone else who might talk—but she won't do it for free."

"Who?" I repeated.

"Leona Brandt," she said. "And she's got the sharpest memory and the longest grudge in Marigold Lake."

Barb groaned. "Leona? That woman could hold a grudge against a saint."

"She also runs the Historical Society," Nanette reminded her. "And she still has copies of the Wexler estate blueprints."

Matt nodded. "It's worth a shot. Claire, can you set up a meeting?"

"I can try," I said, though I knew convincing Leona Brandt to cooperate would be like convincing Sadie to share bacon.

As if on cue, Sadie barked once, clearly disagreeing with my analogy.

"Alright," Matt said, checking his watch. "I'll follow up on Parrish's last known address. You and Nanette talk to Leona. Hannah, see if you can find anything about Reed's involvement in the old Wexler business records."

Barb drained her coffee. "And I'll handle public relations."

I groaned. "Barb—"

"What? Someone has to control the narrative," she said. "Otherwise, by morning we'll be trending under '*Nutmeg Noir.*'"

"Already are," Hannah said cheerfully.

Matt sighed. "I'll meet you back here at sunset. Be careful, Claire."

He left through the front door, and for a moment, the room felt quieter—emptier, almost.

Nanette gave me a look that was equal parts fond and knowing. "He worries about you."

"He worries about everyone," I said.

"Not like that, he doesn't."

Before I could respond, Sadie barked again—this time toward the window. Outside, a black sedan idled at the far end of the street.

Hannah frowned. "That's the same car from yesterday."

The one that had been parked outside the B&B after the last clue arrived.

The car lingered for a moment longer, then pulled away, tires crunching over fallen leaves.

Barb muttered, "Guess we've got fans."

"Or watchers," Nanette said quietly. "Just like before."

I wrapped my arms around myself, staring at the empty street. "Then it's official. The past isn't just knocking—it's moving in."

Sadie pressed against my leg, her little body warm and solid. Outside, the wind caught the marigolds again, scattering petals across the steps like confetti.

Marigold Lake looked peaceful, but I knew better. Somewhere beneath the golden surface, the truth was shifting—and it was only a matter of time before it rose.

Chapter 16

A Pinch of Nutmeg and a Dash of Trouble

The air in Marigold Lake had officially turned crisp. The leaves, no longer clinging stubbornly to their branches, now swirled in vibrant eddies of crimson, gold, and burnt orange. The scent of woodsmoke hung heavy, a comforting reminder that pumpkin spice lattes and cozy sweaters were back in season.

Of course, in my world, "cozy" was usually followed by "mystery" and a healthy dose of chaos.

"Nutmeg," I muttered, staring at the tiny spice rack above my stove. "Seriously? A million-dollar treasure hunt hinges on nutmeg?"

Sadie, perched on her usual lookout post by the back door, let out a disgruntled snort. I knew what she was thinking: *Forget nutmeg—where's the bacon?*

"It's not just the nutmeg, Sadie," I said, grabbing my jacket. "It's where Aunt Teresa got the nutmeg. Matt thinks she might have had a special source."

Matt, bless his logical, detective-y heart, was currently parked outside in his slightly-too-undercover sedan, waiting to whisk me away on our nutmeg-fueled adventure. Hannah, of course, had insisted on joining us, armed with her trusty camera and an arsenal of nutmeg puns that threatened to drive us all insane.

"Okay, team," Hannah announced, bouncing into the kitchen, her blonde ponytail practically vibrating with excitement. "Operation Nutmeg is a go! I already checked Aunt Teresa's grocery lists—no mention of secret suppliers. But I did find a recipe for *Nutmeg Nightmare Cookies.*' Terrifying."

"Let's stick to the treasure hunt," I said, grabbing my purse. "And maybe leave the horror baking for Halloween."

As we piled into Matt's car, I couldn't shake the feeling that we were missing something. The clues had been cryptic, personal. Why lead us to a simple spice? Unless...

"Wait a minute," I said, eyes widening. "What if it's not about where she got the nutmeg, but *when*?"

Matt glanced at me in the rearview mirror. "When?"

"Think about it. The clue said, *'Seek the recipe whispered on bended knee.'* What if Aunt Teresa didn't just buy the nutmeg—what if she received it? As a gift? Or... a message?"

Hannah gasped. "Ooh, like a love potion!"

"Hannah," Matt groaned.

"Okay, not a love potion," I said, grinning. "But maybe it's symbolic. A code. Something tied to the Wexler family."

Matt pulled the car to the side of the road, thinking hard. "That's not a bad theory. So how do we figure out when she started using nutmeg in her muffin recipe?"

"Her journals," I said. "Aunt Teresa kept meticulous journals. Every recipe, every guest, every stray thought."

"Then let's hit the B&B," Matt said, putting the car in gear. "I'll call Nanette—she can help us decipher her handwriting. It always looked like chicken scratch to me."

Back at the Morning Glory, Nanette was already waiting on the porch swing, a stack of Aunt Teresa's journals beside her. Sadie bounded up to greet her, tail wagging, nose to notebook.

"Alright, let's get to work," Nanette said, adjusting her spectacles. "Finding the right nugget of information in these is like searching for a needle in a haystack."

We spent hours flipping through decades of entries. Teresa had recipes for everything from *Anti-Hangover Hash* to *Sadie's Special Salmon Surprise* (which, I suspected, was code for "scraps from dinner"). But no mention of nutmeg.

"This is hopeless," Hannah groaned, rubbing her eyes. "Aunt Teresa wrote about everything except what we need."

"Don't give up yet," I said, turning another brittle page.

Then my eye caught something—a journal entry dated October 27th, 1988. The handwriting was shakier, the ink smudged.

"Wait," I said. "This one's different."

Nanette leaned closer. "Read it."

I did:

Received a most unexpected gift today. A small tin of nutmeg, from a friend I haven't seen in years. A reminder of a promise made, and a secret kept. Perhaps it's time to finally share the Morning Glory Muffin recipe with the world. But only with a special ingredient... a touch of the past.

A hush fell over the porch. The air itself seemed to hold its breath.

"October 27th, 1988," Matt said quietly. "That's the day after Eleanor Wexler disappeared."

The pieces began to click together. The Wexlers. The locket. The nutmeg. Teresa's clue. It wasn't about a recipe—it was about a secret passed down like a coded inheritance.

"We need to find out who gave her that nutmeg," I said. "That's the next key."

Nanette's expression turned solemn. "I might know someone who remembers that day. Someone who knew Eleanor—and the Wexlers—better than anyone."

"Who?" I asked.

She picked up the phone, her hand trembling slightly as she dialed. "It's time," she said softly, "to pay a visit to Colton Parrish."

The name settled over the porch like a chill wind. The last time I'd heard it, it was in one of Teresa's half-finished stories about "the man who disappeared twice."

The lake shimmered beyond the trees, bright and still. But the quiet was deceptive. Somewhere in that reflection, the past was stirring—and it was ready to surface.

Chapter 17

The Mastermind Revealed

THE OLD WEXLER MILL loomed against the bruised purple sky, a skeletal silhouette of rusted metal and decaying wood. The wind howled through broken windows, carrying the hollow wail of forgotten secrets. It was the kind of place that screamed *trespassing* and *bad idea*, but after deciphering the latest clue—a tattered piece of sheet music titled *The Wexler Family Waltz* with a notation marking the mill's coordinates—I was long past caring about caution.

"Remind me again why we're doing this?" Hannah shivered, pulling her scarf tighter. "Because nothing says 'fun Friday night' like breaking into an abandoned death trap."

"Because," I said, adjusting my flashlight beam, "Matt's busy dealing with Gary Mullins's truck and Mrs. Ainsworth's latest petunia catastrophe. And besides..." I hesitated, gazing up at the jagged roofline. "This feels personal. Like Aunt Teresa wanted me to find it."

Sadie let out a low growl, her gaze fixed on the dark doorway ahead. She wasn't fond of creepy buildings—or maybe she just wanted dinner.

"Personal how?" Hannah asked, her voice echoing faintly inside the cavernous structure.

"I don't know yet," I admitted. "But every clue keeps circling back here—to the Wexlers, to Teresa, to this town. It's like the treasure hunt is just a smokescreen for something bigger."

We stepped inside. The floorboards groaned under our weight, and dust swirled in our flashlight beams like dancing ghosts. The air was heavy with the smell of rot and faint traces of oil and metal.

"This place gives me the creeps," Hannah whispered, gripping my arm.

"Me too," I said, though I tried to sound steadier than I felt.

The mill was a labyrinth of rusted machinery, rotting beams, and half-collapsed walls. Each step echoed through the hollow space, and somewhere far above us, a loose sheet of metal clanged against the wind like an offbeat cymbal.

We passed a faded sign that read *Wexler & Sons Timber Co., Est. 1899.* The paint had peeled away, leaving ghost letters that seemed to watch us.

"This is it," I said softly. "The heart of it all."

"More like the horror-movie set of it all," Hannah muttered. "Claire, are you sure about this?"

"No," I said honestly. "But when has that ever stopped me?"

She groaned. "I knew you were going to say that."

A narrow staircase wound up the far wall, its banister eaten away by rust. Sadie sniffed at the first step, then started climbing.

"Let's check the office," I said.

"Or," Hannah countered, "we could not die today."

"Then stay down here," I said, already halfway up.

"Ugh, fine," she sighed, trailing after me. "If I get tetanus, you're paying my medical bills."

We reached the top floor, where the remnants of what must have been the manager's office stood beneath the slanted roof. The space was cluttered with filing cabinets, collapsed desks, and a single broken chair. A long window overlooked the lake, its glass shattered in jagged teeth.

The air felt heavier up there, as if time itself had gathered dust. My flashlight swept across a stack of papers on a desk—receipts, letters, and what looked like a ledger page with Eleanor Wexler's signature. My heart skipped.

Before I could study it further, a voice drifted from the shadows behind us. "I was wondering when you'd show up."

Hannah gasped. I turned, flashlight trembling slightly in my hand.

Colton Parrish stepped into the light. His hair was streaked with gray, his expression calm—too calm. "You really are your aunt's niece," he said. "Always digging where you shouldn't."

"Mr. Parrish," I said, trying to keep my tone even. "We were hoping to talk."

"Talk?" He chuckled. "You've done plenty of talking. Enough to wake up ghosts better left asleep."

Hannah inched closer to me. "You're the one who's been leaving clues?"

He smiled faintly. "Not all of them. I just made sure you followed the right ones."

"Why?" I asked.

"Because Teresa's legacy wasn't yours to uncover," he said. "She made a promise—to protect the truth. To protect *her family*. But you've gone and dug it all up again."

"You mean the Wexlers," I said.

He shook his head slowly. "No, Claire. I mean *you*."

The words hit like ice water.

Hannah's breath caught. "You knew?"

Colton nodded. "Of course. I was there when Eleanor made the deal. Teresa was the insurance—her blood, her choice. Everything she did afterward was to keep you out of it."

"Out of what?" I demanded.

"The balance," he said. "The Wexlers built this town on more than money. They built it on favors—debts that still haven't been paid. Grace Holloway wanted power. I wanted justice. Teresa wanted peace. Now none of us are getting what we wanted."

He moved closer, his voice dropping. "Give me the ledger, and I'll disappear again. This time for good."

"I don't have it," I said. "Matt has it at the station."

Colton's smile vanished. "Then I guess we'll have to adjust the plan."

He reached into his coat—and that's when Sadie lunged.

She moved like a tiny missile, all fur and fury, teeth snapping at Colton's ankles. He shouted, stumbling backward, the gun slipping from his grip. It skittered across the floor and landed at my feet.

Without thinking, I snatched it up and aimed it back at him. My hands trembled, but my voice was steady. "Don't move."

He froze, surprise flickering across his face. "You wouldn't shoot me."

"Try me," I said.

The words came out sharper than I expected. Sadie stood between us, barking furiously. For the first time, Colton looked unsure.

Then, from behind me, a familiar voice cut through the tension. "She won't have to."

Matt burst through the doorway, gun drawn. His gaze locked on Colton. "Put your hands where I can see them."

Colton's sneer faltered, but only for a moment. "Detective Hale," he said, raising his hands slowly. "Right on cue."

Matt crossed the room in two strides, cuffing him with practiced precision. "You have the right to remain silent. I'd recommend it."

As Matt led him toward the stairs, Colton shot me one last look—part anger, part pity. "You think this ends with me?" he said. "You have no idea what your aunt started."

"Save it for your court date," Matt replied, guiding him down the steps.

When they were gone, I finally exhaled. My knees wobbled, and I leaned against the wall. Hannah reached over, grabbing my arm.

"Claire," she said, voice shaking, "you are officially banned from clue-hunting without adult supervision."

Sadie barked once, clearly disagreeing.

I bent down, scooping her up. "Good girl," I whispered. "You just saved the day."

Her tongue darted out to lick my chin, tail wagging with unearned modesty.

By the time we stepped outside, dawn had begun to bleed across the horizon. The lake glowed in the distance, gold and silver ripples breaking the calm surface. For a moment, the world looked soft again, peaceful.

Matt joined us, the faintest smile tugging at his lips. "You really can't help yourself, can you?"

"I was going to call you," I said defensively.

"Uh-huh."

Hannah crossed her arms. "For the record, I voted for calling him."

"Duly noted," Matt said. "And ignored, apparently."

I smiled faintly. "Guess I owe you another batch of muffins."

"You owe me hazard pay," he said, but there was affection behind the words.

As Colton was loaded into the patrol car, he turned his head toward me. "You'll see," he said quietly. "The treasure isn't what you think. You're just another pawn in her game."

"Whose game?" I called.

He didn't answer. The door slammed shut, and the car pulled away, its red taillights vanishing into the fog.

Hannah shivered. "That was unsettling."

"Everything about this week is unsettling," I said. "But at least now we know who's been pulling the strings."

Matt glanced at me. "Maybe. But something tells me there's more to this than Colton Parrish and an old grudge."

I met his gaze, the unease settling in again. "You think someone else was behind him?"

"I think someone was ahead of him," he said quietly.

We stood there in the cool morning air, watching the sunlight spill across the mill's broken façade. The wind had died, the world eerily still.

"Come on," he said finally, wrapping an arm around my shoulders. "Let's go home. We can sort this out after coffee."

"Make it strong," I said.

Back at the Morning Glory, the scent of cinnamon and nutmeg filled the kitchen as I stirred a fresh batch of muffin batter. Hannah hummed distractedly at the sink, and Sadie lay curled on her rug, snoring softly—a tiny hero in retirement.

For a few fleeting minutes, everything felt normal again.

But as I reached for Aunt Teresa's old recipe card, I noticed something I hadn't seen before—faint, purple ink bleeding through the corner.

There was another clue.

And as my pulse quickened, I realized Colton Parrish's words weren't a threat.

They were a warning.

Chapter 18

The Truth Unveiled

TRUDY LOOKED EVERY INCH the social-media star—oversized turtleneck, sparkly leggings, and enough lip gloss to cause glare under the chandelier. Across from her sat Colton Parrish, posture impeccable, expression the picture of wounded nobility.

From my vantage point behind a strategically placed fern, I could see Matt in his slightly-too-small maintenance uniform, fiddling with a flickering light fixture near the front desk. He caught my eye and gave the smallest nod.

The scene could've been comical if the stakes weren't so high.

"So, Mr. Parrish," Trudy said brightly, her phone propped up to record, "my followers are dying to know what brings a man of mystery like you back to Marigold Lake."

He offered a charming, practiced smile. "Just reconnecting with my family's legacy, Ms. Collins. My great-grandfather helped build this town, you know."

"Wow," she said, eyes wide. "Like, literally build it?"

He chuckled. "In a sense. Though some would say the Wexlers took all the credit."

Trudy leaned forward, playing the part perfectly. "So—the Wexlers. You knew them, didn't you?"

His jaw tightened before the smooth smile returned. "I knew *of* them, yes. We all did. The Wexler family was Marigold royalty once upon a time—before greed and gossip took them down."

"Do you think they were guilty?" she asked innocently.

He hesitated a beat. "I think guilt is a matter of who gets to tell the story."

A chill crept over me.

Trudy laughed lightly, twirling her hair. "You sound like a man with secrets."

"I've learned," he said, lowering his voice, "that some truths aren't meant to be uncovered. Not by everyone."

"Can you give me a hint?" she teased.

He smiled, but it didn't reach his eyes. "Let's just say the truth is buried deeper than anyone in this town realizes—and I'm the only one willing to dig it up."

Across the lobby, I saw Matt's hand twitch toward his radio.

Then came the moment that turned the air electric.

Trudy asked softly, "Is it true the Wexler mine still exists?"

Parrish's expression shifted; something feral flickered behind the charm. "Oh, it exists," he said. "And it holds everything this town's been afraid of for forty years."

Before I could process his words, a crash shattered the quiet. Matt had *accidentally* knocked over an entire cart of cleaning supplies. Metal pails clanged against the tile floor, echoing like alarm bells.

"Oops," he said flatly. "Sorry about that."

Every head turned.

Parrish's composure cracked for just a heartbeat—long enough for me to see it: panic. He muttered something under his breath and stood abruptly. "I have to go."

"Mr. Parrish?" Trudy called, but he was already striding toward the exit.

Outside, the wind whipped off the lake, carrying the scent of pine and storm. Matt caught up to him first, calling out, "Colton, wait!"

Parrish spun, eyes wild. "You don't understand. It's not about treasure—it never was."

"Then what is it about?" I demanded, stepping out from behind the door.

He hesitated, torn between defiance and desperation. "Redemption," he said finally. "But the wrong people paid the price."

"Who, Colton?" Matt asked. "Who's still pulling the strings?"

He looked past us, toward the horizon where the lake shimmered like mercury. "You'll see soon enough. She always gets what she wants."

"Grace Holloway," I said.

His silence was answer enough.

Before Matt could reach him, Parrish bolted down the path toward the mill road, vanishing into the line of trees.

Trudy lowered her phone, eyes wide. "Tell me that was *not* live-streaming."

She looked at the screen. "Oh. It was."

Barb's voice crackled through my phone a moment later. "Claire? Why is my newsfeed showing Colton Parrish confessing to crimes in front of Whispering Pines?!"

"Long story," I said, already running after Matt.

We found Parrish half a mile down the road, cornered against a fallen fence line. The glow from Matt's flashlight cut through the dark.

"End of the road, Colton," Matt said evenly.

Parrish raised his hands, breathing hard. "You think I'm the villain here? You have no idea what your precious Detective Hale's been protecting."

"Try me," I said.

He laughed bitterly. "The mine, the money—it was never lost. It was relocated. Your aunt helped move it after the Wexlers fell apart. She hid it beneath the Morning Glory."

I blinked. "That's impossible."

"Check your foundations," he said. "You'll see the truth's been right under your feet."

Before Matt could respond, headlights flooded the road. A black sedan screeched to a stop. Grace Holloway stepped out, calm as ever, a pistol glinting in her hand.

"Enough," she said. "Colton, get in the car."

He froze. "Grace—"

"Now."

Matt moved in front of me. "Put the gun down."

She smiled coldly. "You really think you can stop this, Detective? This town runs on secrets. It always has."

"Not anymore," I said, stepping forward.

Her gaze met mine—steady, assessing. "You're just like her. Teresa thought she could rewrite history too. Tell me, Claire, do you really think the truth will save you?"

"Maybe not," I said. "But it might save everyone else."

For a moment, everything went still—the lake behind us, the air, even the crickets. Then Grace fired.

The shot ricocheted off the metal gatepost, missing Matt by inches. He lunged, tackling her to the ground. The gun skidded into the gravel. Colton dove for it, but Sadie, bless her timing, appeared from the darkness like a four-legged missile, teeth snapping at his sleeve.

Chaos erupted—gravel, shouts, barking. Matt wrestled the weapon away, pinning Grace with one knee. Colton tried to run, but Hannah appeared out of nowhere, wielding a flashlight like a club. "No refunds on this tour!" she yelled, whacking him squarely in the arm.

He yelped, stumbled, and went down.

Matt cuffed them both before they could recover. "You're under arrest for attempted assault, conspiracy, and about a dozen other things I'll enjoy listing later."

Grace glared up at me, her expression unreadable. "You've doomed this town," she said quietly. "The truth will destroy everything the Wexlers built."

"Maybe," I said. "Or maybe it'll finally set it free."

By the time the sirens faded and the last patrol car disappeared down the road, dawn had started to bleed through the trees.

Matt turned to me, weary but smiling. "You all right?"

I nodded. "Tired, sore, and probably banned from Whispering Pines for life—but yeah."

Hannah brushed dirt from her jeans. "Worth it."

Sadie trotted over, tail wagging proudly.

I knelt and rubbed behind her ears. "You, my friend, are getting extra bacon for breakfast."

She barked once, as if to seal the deal.

Matt looked toward the horizon. "You know, for a town obsessed with secrets, Marigold Lake sure knows how to throw an ending."

"Not an ending," I said softly. "Just another chapter."

He smiled. "Then let's hope the next one has fewer gunshots."

"Agreed."

We started back toward the Morning Glory, the first light of morning stretching over the lake, painting everything in gold. The secrets of the Wexlers, the lies, the ledgers—all of it had finally come to the surface.

But as the breeze rippled across the water, I couldn't shake the feeling that Teresa had left one more truth waiting—something deeper still buried in the foundations of the life she built.

And somehow, I knew, it would be up to me to uncover it.

Chapter 19

The Showdown of Wexler's Mine

THE AIR HUNG CRISP and cool, carrying the scent of decaying leaves and woodsmoke—the quintessential Marigold Lake autumn cocktail. Pumpkins perched on stoops, scarecrows slouched like overworked ushers, and the hills blazed with red, orange, and gold. It was the kind of day that begged for cider and a blanket... or, apparently, a confrontation with a potential criminal mastermind.

"Okay, one more time," Matt said, voice tight as the Jeep bounced along a rutted track shouldering into the north woods. Sadie was wedged between us on the bench seat, panting, her eyes flicking from him to me like she was monitoring a very fragile cease-fire. She felt the charge in the air; we all did.

"Colton Parrish," I recited for what had to be the hundredth time. "Former guest at the Morning Glory. Ties to the Wexler scandal. Reappears just as the treasure hunt begins. Disappears between clues. Loves the sound of his own myth."

"And," Matt added, "his prints were on the letters we recovered from Teresa's desk—the ones that mention Richard Reed and the phantom accounts."

Richard Reed. Hannah's grandfather. The mayor's father. Every time the name came up, the universe seemed to tighten a notch.

"So he frames Richard to muddy the water and keep himself clean," I said. "But why the treasure hunt? Why not take whatever's left and vanish?"

"Because money wasn't enough," Matt said, eyes on the road. "He wants control of the story. Revenge. A rewrite, with him positioned as the avenging branch of the 'wronged' family."

"Or," I said, "he's just plain crazy."

"That too," Matt conceded.

The road narrowed to two muddy grooves and spat us into a clearing where the trees opened like curtains. Ahead, built into a low ridge of granite and shale, was the black mouth of the old Wexler Mine: a timbered archway with two cracked warning placards and a sagging gate. To the left, a scattering of loggers' cabins slumped under ropes of ivy; to the right, a rusted winch house leaned like a drunk against the hillside.

Nanette had said this was where the Wexlers' first fortune came out of the ground—cleaner than lumber, dirtier than gold.

"Stay close," Matt said, easing the Jeep behind a tangle of pine to hide it. He checked his radio, then his sidearm. "Backup's fifteen out, maybe more. Market traffic." Only in Marigold Lake would a treasure bust be delayed by preserves and pies.

Sadie gave a low whine. I scratched her ears. "You're the bravest of us," I whispered.

We moved in a tight line across the clearing. Leaves crisped under our boots; crows heckled from the stands of oak. The cabins' windows stared—blank, dark, and too interested.

"Claire." Matt's voice softened without losing its edge. "We don't know what we're walking into."

I nodded once. "Then we walk carefully."

The gate gave with a groan that felt louder than it was, clattering against a chain someone had only pretended to lock. Inside, the mine air changed the world—it was colder by ten degrees and damp enough to taste. Our flashlights sliced long, pale tunnels out of the dark. Faded chalk marks glowed on the timbers every dozen feet, and the old cart rail gleamed like the spine of some sleeping iron creature.

"Left fork," I said. "See the drag marks?" Faint grooves scored the silt. Someone had hauled something heavy not long ago.

"Good eye," Matt murmured, sweeping his beam over the floor. "Boot tread, size eleven. Recent."

We moved. The tunnel sloped down and bent right, then opened into a chamber the size of a small sanctuary. A pile of rotted crates sat against one wall; near the center, a raised frame of beams supported an old hoist platform that looked like it would lose an argument with a strong breeze.

A voice floated out of the shadows, smooth and amused. "We really must stop meeting like this."

Colton Parrish stepped into the circle of my flashlight. The fall of his coat was elegant, but he looked older than the man from the Whispering Pines—eyes rimmed red, jaw tight with sleepless obsession. In his right hand was a small, antique pistol, the sort rich men used to duel when pride outweighed sense.

"Colton," Matt said, the warning barely disguised. "It's over. Put it down."

He smiled like he was humoring a child. "Over? Detective, this is the overture. I've been playing scales for forty years."

"You staged a town-wide treasure hunt to settle a grudge," I said. "You endangered half the population and an entire bed of Mrs. Ainsworth's petunias."

He didn't blink. "The petunias had it coming."

I took a step forward; Sadie matched me. "You framed a family to erase your own guilt. You used my aunt's legacy to stir the past with a dirty spoon. Why?"

His smile cooled. "Because they stole everything from us. The deals that should've been ours. The praise. The future. Do you know what it's like to walk through a town built on your family's bones?" He gestured at the darkness around us. "This—this is Wexler blood."

"Blood doesn't excuse cruelty," I said.

"Cruelty?" He laughed, short and bright, the sound skittering up the timbers. "You think I broke a few laws and we're even? Your aunt—Teresa—hid the proof that would have restored what we lost. She chose the town." He tilted his head. "What will you choose?"

Sadie's growl vibrated against my shin. Matt shifted his stance a fraction, angling to draw Colton's eye. "Hands where I can see them."

"Ah, Detective," Colton said lightly. "Still playing by rules that were written by liars."

He moved—too fast for sense. The barrel came up.

Sadie launched.

She hit his ankle like a furry meteor, teeth flashing. Colton shouted and flinched hard with the shock; the pistol went wide and fired into the dark with a crack that ricocheted down every tunnel like a scream. In the same instant, Matt lunged, caught

Colton's wrist, twisted—steel clanged across the rock floor and vanished off the platform, rattling into a lower shaft.

Everything held its breath for one sick heartbeat. Then the mine decided it was time to participate.

A tremor rattled the frame. Dust sifted down in silver sheets. A plank on the hoist platform groaned.

"Move!" Matt snapped.

We dove off the platform as a support beam shuddered and dropped a fraction. A rope that had been lazily looped through the pulley wheel above shrieked through the iron throat—weight shifted somewhere in the black, and something heavy thumped. I rolled, caught Sadie against my stomach, and scrambled to my knees as the platform coughed up a board and spat it into the chamber like a very large, very unhappy tongue depressor.

Colton bucked under Matt's weight, furious and slippery, and for a moment he almost twisted free. But Sadie—god bless her tiny, chaotic soul—came around again and latched onto the cuff of Colton's coat with a snarl audible in three counties. He yanked instinctively to shake her; it bought Matt the half-second he needed. The cuffs clicked with a satisfaction that sounded louder than the gunshot had.

"It's over," Matt said, breathing hard. "Don't argue."

Colton went still, his chest rising and falling fast, fury burning like frost in his eyes. "You think this ends with me?" he panted. "You think I'm the only one who wanted the truth chained in a hole?"

"Stand up," Matt said. He did, hands secured behind him, jaw set like stone.

"Claire," Matt murmured, "you okay?"

"Fine," I said, which was only mostly a lie. "Sadie?"

She wagged, feathers of dust clinging to her whiskers like glitter.

"Good girl," I whispered, burying my face for a second in her warm neck. When I looked up, the chamber felt slightly less like a tomb.

Colton smiled again, slow, terrible. "You're so proud of your little victory. But you haven't found what matters."

"We found enough," I said.

"Have you?" He leaned, conspiratorial, the cuffs chinking. "There's a door. Teresa knew about it. She wrote about it in ink that stains like regret. Find the door, Keeper of Memories. Then we'll see if you still prefer the truth."

A clatter sounded from the right-hand tunnel—pebbles skipping, footsteps slapping rock. I whipped my light that direction, expecting the rest of the cavalry or a rotten log. A shape flashed past at the edge of the beam. Not a deputy. Smaller. Quicker. A woman in a dark jacket, hair pulled tight. Gone before I registered her face.

"Did you—" I started.

"I saw," Matt said, all business again. "We're not alone."

He moved Colton toward the archway. The mine creaked another opinion; somewhere to our left a beam gave up the ghost with a tired sigh. The message was clear: time to vacate.

We half-jogged the last bend, the daylight at the mouth of the tunnel a square of promise. Outside, the sky had shifted to late afternoon; mist was forming along the treeline, a pale beast stalking the pines. We hustled Colton into the open and toward the Jeep.

"Backup?" I asked.

"Two minutes," Matt said. "ETA more like five."

A twig snapped near the winch house. I turned just as a shadow peeled itself away from the slats. The woman from the tunnel stepped out, not quite pointing a gun, but not *not* pointing it—chin lifted, posture ballerina-straight.

"Careful, Detective," she called. "Wouldn't want all your hard work to go to waste."

The voice prickled at something in my memory. Then she stepped closer and the light caught her face.

Grace Holloway.

Of course. Of course the woman who'd broken into my house like an autumn draft would pop up at the mine's curtain call.

Her gaze flicked over me, unimpressed. "You run very loud investigations, Ms. Fisher. It's a miracle anything in this town stays buried."

Colton laughed softly, almost sweetly. "Grace. Late as ever."

She ignored him. "You have something that doesn't belong to you."

"If you mean a suspect in custody," Matt said, "we're attached."

"I mean the evidence," she said. "The ledger. The letters. The parts of the story that keep the town livable."

I took one step forward. "Livable for who?"

"For everyone," she said crisply, like she was correcting a child. "You think truth is disinfectant. But stories hold towns together, Ms. Fisher. Not facts. Not accounting. Stories. You crack the wrong seam, and the whole thing collapses."

Matt angled his body, unobtrusive and deliberate, to keep both her and Colton in his sightline. "Put the gun down."

Her eyes cooled. "No. You're going to give me what Teresa promised me years ago—a chance to keep this town from eating itself."

Colton snorted. "There it is. The Reed apologist."

Her attention snapped to him, and for a heartbeat the mask slipped. "I apologize for nothing," she said softly. "I protect."

A second siren wound thinly through the trees. She heard it too. Calculus ticked behind her eyes. She took a half-step back into shadow, and when she spoke again, her voice was almost kind. "Walk away, Claire. You won't like what you find on the other side of the door."

Then she was gone—melted into the timber and vine as if the woods themselves had invited her in.

"Door?" Matt said under his breath.

"Teresa mentioned a door in one of her letters," I said, memory sliding into place like a key. "A door that 'doesn't ask nicely.' I thought it was metaphor."

"Maybe not," Matt said.

Two cruisers bumped into the clearing, their tires crunching stellated leaves. Relief hit like a second wind. Officers took Colton from Matt's custody with the efficient gentleness of people who do one dangerous thing very carefully for a living. He didn't resist; he looked almost pleased.

As they guided him toward the back seat, he turned his head and found me. "We're almost finished, Keeper," he said softly. "Tell your aunt I kept my promise."

The door shut. The cruiser pulled away, lightbar dark. The forest exhaled. Or maybe I did.

I stood there for a moment with my hands in my pockets and the breath of the mine on my face. Sadie pressed her flank to my calf, solid as an oath. Matt touched my elbow, grounding.

"You did good," he said.

"So did you. And Sadie deserves a steak."

"Non-negotiable."

We should have felt victorious, and maybe some small part of me did—because Sadie was safe, because a man who had terrified me for weeks was finally cuffed and driven off under a sky that wasn't sure yet if it wanted to snow. But my pulse didn't slow. Grace's voice kept brushing the edges of my mind like cold water. *Find the door. Don't open it.*

"Claire?" Matt asked.

"I want to look at the platform again," I said. "Quickly. Before anyone seals this place off."

He weighed that for a second, then nodded. "Two minutes. And we stay together."

"Deal."

Back into the lungs of the hill. Back past the chalk marks and the whisper of dust. In the hoist chamber, the platform sulked, tilted and splintered where it had bucked. The pulley rope still hung in a lazy loop.

"Look," I said. On the far support, near a knot in the timber, someone had carved a small, awkward heart with a nail. Not the elegant script from the letters. A child's hand. Beneath it, barely visible beneath decades of grime, a crude arrow pointed down.

Matt crouched, sweeping his light along the base of the frame. "Panel," he said. "Loose."

He pried gently with his multitool. The board shifted, then popped, revealing a shallow cavity barely the size of a shoebox. Inside was a metal envelope—the kind surveyors used—sealed with a strip of wax gone brittle with time. In the wax, the impression of that same naïve heart. Not Wexler. Not Reed. Not Teresa. Someone else's stubborn hope pressed into red.

My throat felt tight in a way that had nothing to do with cold air. I didn't touch it. Not yet.

"Let the lab open it," Matt said quietly, as if reading the battle on my face.

"I know," I said. I also knew it was killing me.

He slid the envelope into an evidence bag. I closed my eyes for a second, then opened them again on the fracture lines of the old wood, the scuffs of boots, the ghost of a map. The mine creaked—less angry now, more curious.

"Okay," I said. "Let's go home."

Outside, evening had pressed the color out of the sky, leaving the last leaves to shine like lamps where they clung. The cruisers were gone, the clearing half-empty and echoing. We climbed into the Jeep. Sadie turned three circles and collapsed with a sigh so dramatic it should've had its own credit line.

As we bumped back toward town, lights began to wink on in the distance—porch by porch, window by window—until Marigold Lake looked like it had set the stars at table height. Somewhere in that soft glow, people were stirring soup and untangling yarn and arguing gently about who cheated at Bingo. The kind of normal that uses both hands.

"What now?" I asked.

"Now," Matt said, "we book Parrish. We log the mine evidence. We write the most boring reports imaginable so a very not-boring case holds in court. And then—" He glanced at me, a half-smile there and gone. "We find your door."

I rested my head against the cold window. "We find it together."

"Together," he echoed.

Back at the Morning Glory, the kitchen light was a small sun. Barb met us at the door with a casserole like it was armor. Hannah barreled in behind her, eyes scanning for blood, then relaxing into relief when she saw all our limbs present and accounted for. There were hugs, and the kind of bickering that means love, and Sadie paraded through the living room like a war hero who would absolutely accept tributes of bacon.

But when the house quieted—after the casserole and the updates and the three separate retellings of Sadie's flying leap—I found myself alone in Aunt Teresa's office, the roll-top desk open, her lavender-scented drawers breathing out comfort. On top of the blotter lay the ledger, safely bagged and tagged; beside it, my copy of Teresa's journal, ribbon fading to gray.

I slid into the chair and opened to the page I suspected had been waiting for me.

There is a door in every town, Teresa had written in a hand that hurried and then corrected itself. *Some open onto light, and some onto storms. If you have to open the storm-door, do it with friends at your back and a good dog at your feet. And remember, Claire: the truth is not a wrecking ball. It is a key. Use it to unlock, not to destroy.*

I closed the journal and laid my palm across the words until warmth bled through ink.

From the hallway, Matt's voice drifted, low and steady. Hannah's laughter fizzed in reply. Sadie snored on the rug like a tiny freight train.

Tomorrow we'd tell the town. Tomorrow we'd open the metal envelope. Tomorrow we'd go looking for a door that might prefer to stay shut.

Tonight, we kept the lights on.

And if the wind outside the Morning Glory sounded like it was playing a familiar waltz, well—maybe that was just the mine exhaling, relieved that, finally, someone had listened.

Chapter 20

The Papers in the Walls

THE AIR IN MARIGOLD Lake crackled with an autumn chill, mirroring the tension that had taken root in my stomach. Leaves the color of burnt orange and angry crimson swirled around my ankles as Matt and I stood before the wrought-iron gates of the old Wexler estate. The place loomed at the end of a long, overgrown drive like a guilty conscience.

"Are you sure about this, Claire?" Matt ran a hand through his dark blond hair—never a great sign. "Feels like walking into a trap."

"It probably is," I said, tugging Aunt Teresa's paisley scarf tighter where it clashed merrily with my floral dress. "But we're out of time. This is where the paper trail ends. Teresa's notes point here. So did Harold the postman's gossip when he thought impressing Leona Brandt might lead to romance." I paused. "It won't. But he did give us a useful tip."

Sadie huffed at a maple leaf, unimpressed by either romance or tips.

The "mishaps" had been escalating—Finn's ladder "slipped," someone brought lemon bars to Bunco that could strip paint, and Nanette's brake line looked like it had met a very small, very dedicated mouse with wire cutters. The humor quotient was plummeting. Whoever was left on the board wanted the endgame, now.

"We move together," Matt said, voice low. "Eyes up. And Sadie—minimal heroics unless absolutely necessary."

Sadie's look said she'd make that call herself.

The gates complained open. We crunched up a drive half-swallowed by weeds until the Wexler house presented itself in all its Gothic melodrama: stone bruised by weather, windows black as a shut piano, gables that looked like they sprouted bats on command. Cobwebs had taken up interior design.

"Charming," I muttered.

We crossed the threshold, and the smell changed—mothballs, damp plaster, and the old, papery exhale of a house that remembered being loved. Dust motes floated in the angled light like tiny stage cues. Somewhere in the walls, something settled with the resigned sigh of ancient timber.

"Hello?" I called, letting my voice carry—not taunting, not timid. "We're not here to break anything. We just want the truth."

Silence. Then a distant creak that could have been a floorboard or a ghost with bunions.

"Library," Matt said. "Records would live there if they lived anywhere."

It looked like a storm had tried to alphabetize it. Shelves sagged under the weight of neglected spines, a ladder leaned at an angle that suggested it enjoyed causing lawsuits, and in the fireplace, a heap of ash had been swept into a careful cone. I ran a finger along a row of leather-bound novels until one, fatter and less dusty than its neighbors, caught my eye.

"Wuthering Heights," I said. "Of course."

I slid it free. Something fluttered to the rug—a slip of yellowed paper. The ink had bled into the fibers like tears.

Meet me at the Whispering Pines, by the old willow. I have news about the deed. —R.

"1928," I breathed, reading the faded date. "The willow. The first clue. This was never a game—it was a breadcrumb trail from the beginning."

A floorboard whispered behind me. I turned, heart climbing into my throat.

"Looking for something, Claire?"

Grace Holloway stepped out of the doorway's shadow, the light catching the calm severity of her profile. She held a small pistol with the casual familiarity of someone who had decided long ago that necessity outranked scruples. In the set of her shoulders I saw the same iron that had driven her to slide purple-ink notes under my door and ghost through my attic like a winter draft.

"Ms. Holloway," I said, keeping my voice level. "Colton's in custody. You're late to the party."

She didn't look at the gun, didn't look at my hands. Her attention flicked around the room as if counting exits, then came back to me with a tired kind of pity. "Parrish is a symptom. The town's disease is older."

"Is that what we're calling forgery and sabotage?" I said. "Symptoms?"

"Balance," she said. "The Reeds kept this place alive when scandal could have killed it. The Wexlers are not villains. But if you throw the wrong stones at the wrong time, all you do is shatter windows."

"Truth isn't a stone," I said, hearing Teresa in my own words. "It's a key."

Grace's mouth twitched—annoyance or the ghost of a smile. "Teresa said that too. Right before she gave me her key." She reached into her coat with her free hand and drew out a small brass heart—the twin of the one we'd found in the clock at the Morning Glory. "She wanted to keep the peace. So do I."

"By what—burning the evidence?" I nodded at the fireplace.

Her gaze slid toward the ash. "We all choose the fires we can live with."

"Where are the papers?" I asked softly.

"In the walls," she said, and for a heartbeat the severity softened into something like wonder. "The Wexler women hid more than letters. They hid grief and stubbornness and the only proof that could unmake a dynasty. And then they hid the map to it in library cards and recipe margins and waltz annotations because no one ever looks where women keep things."

"Women do," I said.

She inclined her head. "Exactly."

A quiet step sounded in the hall. Grace's attention flicked toward it, fast as a bird. Matt's silhouette slid into the threshold, his gun low, his voice steady. "Ms. Holloway. That's enough."

Her jaw hardened. "Detective. Always a pleasure."

"Put it down," he said. "We're done waving weapons in historic properties."

"This is not yours to decide," she said. "If you open the wrong door, you won't recognize your town when you're finished."

"Then let the town decide," I said. "Not one person with a pistol and a tidy story."

She studied me, the weight of a hundred calculations in a single, measured inhale. "You think the truth will save you. Maybe it will. Or maybe it will take everything you love and grind it into a morality tale." Her eyes cooled. "Teresa understood that. She loved this town more than she loved being right."

"She loved both," I said. "She found a way to make them the same."

Something like grief rippled across Grace's face and was gone. "Then prove it."

We moved together, a slow triangle of intent. Matt's focus never left the pistol. Grace's never left my hands. And mine were busy with the shelves—scanning edges, looking for repeats, the places a librarian's order rubbed awkwardly against a hider's haste.

There. A run of law texts, 1910 through 1915—then a gap, then 1917. "What happened to 1916?"

"It went to war," Grace said dryly.

I pressed my palm to the panel behind the gap. It was cooler than its neighbors. The faintest ridge kissed my fingertips. "Here," I said.

"Claire," Matt warned.

"Cover me," I said, and tried not to think about how very often those words had preceded regrettable choices. I hooked my nails under the molding, wiggled, and felt the give—old glue sighing, a secret stretching after a long nap. The trim lifted, then popped. A narrow door the height of my forearm swung inward on hidden pins.

Behind it lay a cavity stuffed to the seams with flat bundles wrapped in oilcloth and tied with string gone crisp with age. My breath went small and useless. I slid one out. The string cracked. The oilcloth unfurled and released the smell of ink and cedar and something like lightning.

Inside: ledgers, copies of deeds, letters—so many letters—photographs whose silvering had turned the edges to twilight. A title leapt at me in a stern, neat hand: *Conveyance of Mill and Water Rights, Reed to Wexler, 1928.* Beneath it, a second document: *Reversal and Forfeiture, Wexler to Reed, 1931.* The signatures didn't match. In the margin of the second, a note in a woman's hand: *He signed with his left.*

"Reginald was right-handed," I whispered.

Matt's light slid over the page. "And Richard Reed learned to sign with either after he broke his wrist in '31. Nanette told me that yesterday."

Grace's gun didn't waver, but her shoulders sagged the smallest degree. "You think a forged signature fifty years ago fixes anything now?"

"It fixes a name," I said, eyes burning. "It fixes who we blame at Sunday dinner."

Her face shut. "Blame is a luxury."

"Truth is not," Matt said calmly. "Ms. Holloway, set the weapon down. Now."

For a heartbeat I thought she'd refuse. Then, as if a bell only she could hear had tolled once and for all, she lowered the pistol and nudged it toward Matt with the toe of her boot.

"Do you think I wanted this?" she asked me, not looking away. "Do you think I wanted to spend my life patching holes in stories so children wouldn't fall through them?"

"I think you mistook silence for kindness," I said, and tried to make it gentler than it felt. "And you're not the only one."

A small, outraged bark exploded at our ankles. Sadie, who had been a model of restraint for a full five minutes, decided her moment had come. She launched at Grace's hem and seized it like it owed her money. In the startled shuffle that followed, Matt stepped in, scooped the pistol fully away, and collected the brass key from Grace's palm. He holstered one, bagged the other, and exhaled.

"Thank you," he said, and meant it. "Let's do this the right way."

For once, Grace didn't argue.

We worked quickly—evidence bags, photos, the careful listing of line and seal that turns history into something a judge will recognize. I found more notes in that sharp woman's hand, clipped to affidavits and phone bills: *He wasn't at the mill that night. He was at the hall, calling the dance.* A grainy photograph of Eleanor Wexler under the willow, posture bright with joy. A receipt stamped with a date that cut clean through an old rumor's throat.

The last oilcloth bundle held a single envelope sealed in purple wax with a clumsy little heart—nothing like the elegant W we'd been taunted by. I broke it with a breath I couldn't quite take.

If you have found this, then the last lie has broken, the letter read in Teresa's looping hand. *The evidence belongs to the town. The story belongs to everyone. Don't let either belong to one family again—ours or theirs. Put it in the light, Claire. And then make muffins.*

Tears blurred the ink. "Bossy to the end," I said, smiling wetly.

"Wise to the end," Nanette said from the doorway.

I turned. She stood with Leona in her wake and Harold peeking over Leona's shoulder with the wide-eyed look of a man who'd stumbled into a confession booth. Barb was there too, clutching a thermos like it could be weaponized if necessary. Hannah rushed past them and took the stack of photographs from my hands as if she'd been waiting her whole life to catch them.

"How did—" I began.

"Small town," Barb said. "You left your porch light on."

Leona's mouth was set, but her eyes had gone soft at the edges. "We'll do this properly," she said briskly. "Chain of custody. Copies for the Historical Society. An exhibit, once the dust settles, because healing requires a place to stand and look."

Nanette came to my side and squeezed my elbow. "You did it, Keeper," she whispered. "You brought it all home."

Grace stood very straight, hands visible, chin lifted like a woman who has decided to meet consequences on her feet. "I'll give a statement," she said. "The truth, this time. Even the parts that make me look small."

"Thank you," I said, and meant that, too.

We emerged onto the front steps carrying the past in plastic and twine. The wind lifted the last leaves into a clatter that sounded almost like applause. Down the drive, the first curious neighbors had already started to collect—two teenagers on bikes, Mrs. Ainsworth in a shawl dramatic enough to deserve a solo, Finn with a smudge of grease on his cheek and worry in his eyes. The crowd made space for us like the sea learning manners.

Mayor Reed stood near the gate, hat in hand, as if he'd practiced remorse in the mirror and then hated the way it looked on him. "Ms. Fisher," he said hoarsely. "Detective. Ms. Holloway. I... if there's been a wrongdoing—"

"There was," Leona said crisply, and saved him from the rest.

I looked at Hannah, at Nanette, at Matt. At Sadie, who had planted herself squarely on the top step as if declaring eminent domain for dogs who do brave things. "We have documents," I said, loud enough for the crowd without shouting. "They show that the Wexler family didn't steal what they were accused of. And they show who did."

A ripple went through the gathered faces—not shock so much as relief with a chaser of sorrow. Because truth never arrives alone. It brings the bill.

"We'll release what we can as soon as possible," Matt added. "There will be a formal statement. For now, go home. Be kind to each other. This is still the same town you loved yesterday."

Barb lifted the thermos like a toast. "And there's chili at the church hall. Because justice is hungry work."

Laughter, thin and grateful, fluttered across the porch. People began to drift in ones and twos, voices low, eyes bright.

Mayor Reed didn't move until we reached him. He looked at the plastic-wrapped pages as if they were a verdict and a pardon in one. "I'll cooperate," he said quietly. "Whatever's needed."

"That's a good start," Matt said.

Back at the Morning Glory, we spread Teresa's letter and the first copies on the kitchen island while chili warmed and people who loved each other argued about whether cinnamon belonged in it. The house filled with the familiar orchestra—Hannah clattering spoons, Barb narrating everything for posterity, Nanette humming under her breath like a kettle coming to boil. Even Leona allowed herself a smile so small it might have been an accident.

I pulled out the muffin tins.

"Really?" Hannah asked, half teasing, half tender. "Now?"

"Teresa's orders," I said. "Put it in the light. Then make muffins."

As the batter slid into its cups and the oven door thunked gently shut, the weight in my chest began to rearrange itself into something I could carry. Sadie curled at my feet, blissfully asleep, one ear cocked as if the house itself were telling her a bedtime story.

An hour later, we walked the first tray down to the church hall. The town was already there—of course it was—people holding paper bowls, holding hands, holding complicated feelings with the grace of practice. We set the muffins on a table draped with a crocheted runner someone's great-aunt had made during a winter that would not end.

I stood beside Matt and looked out at Marigold Lake—flawed and stubborn and ours. We had put the treasure in the only place it could do any good: where everyone could see it. Tomorrow would be hard. The day after might be harder. But the road home is still a road.

"Hey," Matt said softly, his shoulder against mine. "You okay?"

I breathed in flour and cinnamon and the steady hum of a room deciding to heal. "Not yet," I said. "Soon."

He nodded, as if *soon* were a promise we could keep.

Across the room, Grace sat between Nanette and Leona, answering quiet questions with quiet honesty. Mayor Reed poured coffee and didn't pretend he was anyone but a man learning his family wasn't made of marble. Finn found Hannah's hand and didn't let go. Barb circulated with a pad of paper, taking notes like a friendly spy.

And when the first muffin tray came back empty, I realized Teresa had been right all along. The treasure was never gold. It was a town that could face the truth, feed each other anyway, and find a way to keep dancing.

Outside, the wind lifted, and the last marigolds along the fence nodded as if satisfied. Tomorrow would bring statements and headlines and meetings that smelled like photocopier toner. But tonight, we had sugar and nutmeg and the soft clatter of plates.

We had the light on.
We had each other.

Chapter 21

The Mill at Midnight

THE AIR IN MARIGOLD Lake crackled with tension thicker than Mrs. Ainsworth's stage makeup. The revelation that Colton Parrish—the charming but enigmatic guest who'd stayed at the Morning Glory just weeks ago—was the mastermind behind the treasure hunt had sent shockwaves through town. The fact that he was also Eleanor Wexler's grandson only fueled the fire.

"I can't believe it," Hannah said, pacing the kitchen like a caffeinated hummingbird. "Colton? He seemed so... normal! Well, normal for someone who collects antique thimbles, anyway."

Sadie whined softly, pressing her nose against my leg. I crouched down, giving her a scratch behind the ears. "I know, girl. It's a lot to take in."

Matt stood by the window, arms folded, the reflection of flashing police lights from Main Street glinting in his eyes. He'd been uncharacteristically quiet since Colton's confession. "We need to figure out his next move," he said finally. "He admitted to orchestrating the treasure hunt to clear his grandmother's name, but that doesn't explain the sabotage."

"You mean Gary's brakes and the B&B's wiring fiasco?" I asked, my stomach twisting. "He wouldn't actually hurt anyone... would he?"

Matt's jaw tightened. "Desperation makes people do crazy things."

Barb Wetherly, who had been unusually subdued, spoke up from her stool. "I always knew there was something shifty about that Colton Parrish. Too smooth, too charming—just like his grandfather, Richard Wexler."

I sighed. "Great. More Wexler family drama."

"This is bigger than drama, Claire," Nanette Caldwell said, adjusting her glasses. "It's about justice. Eleanor Wexler was wrongly accused, and Colton was determined to set the record straight. He just... chose the wrong way."

Before anyone could respond, the phone rang—shrill, urgent, slicing through the tension like a knife. I snatched it up. "Morning Glory B&B, Claire speaking."

"Claire, it's Mayor Reed." His voice was frantic. "Colton Parrish is at the old Wexler Lumber Mill. He's barricaded himself inside, and he's threatening to... to..."

My pulse spiked. "To what, Mayor?"

"To blow the whole place up!" he blurted. "He says he's going to expose the truth one way or another!"

I slammed the phone down, heart racing. "He's at the lumber mill. He's threatening to blow it up."

Matt didn't hesitate. He grabbed his keys. "Let's go."

The autumn wind whipped through my hair as we sped toward the outskirts of town. The Wexler Lumber Mill loomed ahead, its rusted roofline cutting a jagged silhouette against the dusky sky. Once the heartbeat of Marigold Lake's industry, it had long since fallen into ruin—a monument to secrets and decay.

When we arrived, the scene was chaos. Police cars and fire trucks ringed the property, their lights flashing red and blue across the cracked asphalt. Officers moved with controlled urgency, setting up barricades and ushering onlookers back. The air smelled like smoke, metal, and fear.

Mayor Reed was pacing near the entrance, his face pale. He spotted us and hurried over. "Detective Hale—thank goodness. He won't talk to anyone. He's locked himself inside with some kind of detonator. Keeps shouting about Eleanor and a ledger that will 'prove everything.'"

Matt nodded grimly. "I'll talk to him. Keep everyone back."

I opened my mouth to protest, but one look at Matt told me there was no arguing. He was in full detective mode—steady, focused, impossible to sway. He approached the mill slowly, hands raised.

"Colton, it's Matt Hale," he called out. "No one wants to hurt you. We just want to talk."

For a long, agonizing moment, there was silence. Then a distorted voice boomed from the building's old intercom system, metallic and trembling with anger. "Stay back! I won't let them silence me like they silenced my grandmother!"

"Colton, no one's trying to silence you," Matt said, his tone calm and even. "But blowing up the mill won't clear her name—it'll only destroy what's left of it."

"It's the only way they'll listen!" Colton shouted. "They covered up the truth for decades. They ruined my family. Now they'll pay!"

I clutched Sadie's leash tighter, my heart thudding in my chest. Matt kept his voice measured, but Colton's tone had the brittle edge of someone teetering on the brink.

Then Sadie barked—a sharp, insistent sound that cut through the noise. She wasn't looking at the mill; she was staring off to the side, toward a narrow, overgrown trail that disappeared into the trees. Her tail stiffened.

"What is it, girl?" I whispered.

She barked again, pulling at the leash. I followed her gaze—and saw a faint glint of light at the back of the mill.

"Matt!" I called. "There's another way in. I'm going to check it out."

His head snapped toward me, alarm flashing in his eyes. "Claire—no. Wait for backup."

"Just keep him talking," I said, already moving. "I'll be careful."

"Claire!"

But I was gone, Sadie leading the way through the thicket. The trail was narrow, choked with weeds and brambles. Twigs snapped underfoot, and my scarf caught on a low branch as if trying to hold me back.

The path ended at a small service door, half-hidden behind ivy. Sadie sniffed at it, then looked up expectantly.

"You've got better instincts than half the police department," I murmured.

I gripped the rusted handle. It turned with a protesting squeal. The door creaked open into darkness.

The smell hit me first—old wood, oil, and dust thick enough to taste. Faint light filtered through cracked boards. Somewhere above, Colton's voice echoed, distant but furious.

Sadie stayed close to my ankle as I crept down the corridor. My flashlight beam trembled over machinery, broken crates, and piles of lumber.

Then we reached a side room—and there, on a table blanketed in dust, sat a thick leather ledger. Its pages were yellowed, its cover embossed with a faded **W**.

The hidden ledger. The key to Eleanor Wexler's innocence.

I stepped closer, heart pounding. My fingers brushed the cover—

"Don't touch that."

I froze. The voice came from the doorway behind me.

Colton Parrish stood there, his face streaked with grime, his eyes wild. In one hand he held a small detonator.

"Colton," I said quietly, raising my hands. "You don't need to do this."

"It's the only way," he said hoarsely. "They stole everything from us—our name, our honor. My grandmother died branded a thief."

"But blowing this place up won't bring her justice," I said. "Look." I pointed to the ledger. "This can. This proves everything. Let me take it to Matt. Let us show the truth."

He hesitated, the detonator trembling in his hand. "You promise?"

"I promise," I said, taking a slow step forward. "Let me help you. Please."

For a moment, he looked like a lost boy again—torn between fury and hope. Then, with a shaky breath, he lowered the detonator.

"Okay," he whispered.

Relief flooded me so fast it made my knees weak. I reached for the ledger—

And he lunged.

His hand clamped around my wrist, his grip bruising. "But if you're lying," he hissed, eyes blazing, "I'll make you pay."

Sadie growled, low and steady. The air crackled between us—dust motes, fear, and the faint click of the detonator still poised in his other hand.

"Colton," I said softly, meeting his gaze. "If I was lying, I'd have brought an army instead of a Boston Terrier."

That gave him pause—just enough.

Outside, I heard Matt shouting my name. Tires screeched. The hum of a megaphone echoed: "Colton Parrish, this is your last chance!"

Colton's face twisted in anguish. "They'll never understand," he muttered.

"Then let me help them," I said. "Let me finish what your grandmother started."

His hand trembled. For one terrifying second, I thought he'd press the button—then, slowly, he let the detonator drop to the floor.

It clattered against the concrete.

I exhaled shakily, reaching for Sadie, who barked once—as if announcing victory.

Matt appeared in the doorway seconds later, gun drawn, eyes blazing. "Claire! You okay?"

"Define okay," I said, my heart still hammering.

Matt cuffed Colton without resistance. "It's over," he told him.

"No," Colton said softly, his voice hollow. "It's just beginning. You'll see."

As they led him outside, I held the ledger to my chest, the weight of it both literal and heavy with history. The air outside was thick with relief and sirens.

Mayor Reed looked stricken as Colton passed. "Good Lord... I had no idea—"

"Maybe that's been the problem all along," I said quietly.

Matt glanced at me, his expression softening. "You could've been killed."

"Maybe," I said, looking down at Sadie, who was trotting proudly at my side. "But then who would've found the ledger?"

He gave me that look—the half-exasperated, half-admiring one I was starting to know by heart.

"Come on," he said. "Let's get that evidence somewhere safe before you decide to chase another clue."

That night, the Morning Glory glowed warm against the chill creeping in from the lake. I sat at the kitchen table with the ledger open before me, its ink faded but legible. Each page told a story—names, numbers, signatures, and finally, the proof that Eleanor Wexler had been framed to cover another man's greed.

Sadie snored softly at my feet. Matt poured two cups of coffee and set one in front of me.

"Well," he said, sitting down across from me, "you were right again."

"Don't sound so surprised," I said, smiling tiredly.

He leaned back, watching me over the rim of his mug. "You realize this isn't just a treasure hunt anymore, right?"

"Oh, I know," I said. "It's a reckoning."

I turned another page. Somewhere in the margin, in a graceful hand that might have been Eleanor's, someone had written a single line: *Truth endures.*

Outside, the wind rattled the porch swing, and the lake whispered like it always does after a storm. The worst was over—or so I hoped. But in Marigold Lake, even the truth had a way of stirring up more secrets.

And I had a feeling we weren't done yet.

Chapter 22

The Truth in the Ledger

THE MORNING AFTER THE mill incident dawned crisp and calm, as if Marigold Lake itself had exhaled after holding its breath all night. Mist hovered over the water, drifting lazily toward shore, and the air smelled faintly of apples and woodsmoke.

Inside the Morning Glory, however, calm was still a work in progress.

Nanette sat at the dining room table, a steaming mug of chamomile in one hand and her spectacles perched low on her nose as she flipped carefully through the leather-bound ledger. Barb hovered behind her with a notebook labeled *Community Crisis Notes (Vol. 2)*, ready to document anything scandal-worthy. Hannah stood near the bay window, arms crossed tightly, her normally sunny expression clouded with unease.

Sadie, the only one seemingly unaffected, snored softly under the table, her paw twitching as if she were chasing rabbits—or possibly muffin crumbs.

I poured another round of coffee and joined the group. "How far have we gotten?"

Nanette sighed. "Page seventy-four. It's not easy to decipher. Half the entries are written in shorthand, and the ink's faded in places. But it's clear enough to know this ledger is... significant."

Barb leaned in. "Significant how? Town-hall-scandal significant or national-news significant? Because I have very different fonts for those."

"More like truth-restoring significant," Nanette said. "This ledger tracks financial transfers from the lumber company to a private account—one belonging to Richard Reed. It shows how he forged Eleanor Wexler's signature to make it look like she'd embezzled funds."

A heavy silence filled the room. The only sound was the soft clink of Sadie's collar as she shifted in her sleep.

"So it's true," Hannah whispered finally. "My great-grandfather framed her."

I moved closer and touched her arm. "Yes. But it's also proof that Eleanor was innocent. Colton wasn't wrong to want justice—he just lost himself in how to find it."

Hannah blinked rapidly, her blue eyes glistening. "I grew up hearing my family talk about how the Wexlers ruined us. How my great-grandfather was a victim. And all this time..." Her voice broke. "He was the one who did the ruining."

Matt, standing quietly in the doorway, crossed the room and set a hand on her shoulder. "It doesn't define you, Hannah. You've done more good for this town in one Bunco night than he did in his lifetime. And now, thanks to Claire, Nanette, and Sadie, the truth can finally come out."

Barb sniffed. "And it's about time. I can only rewrite history in my gossip column so many times before people start fact-checking me."

Hannah gave a watery laugh. "Leave it to you to find a silver lining in family scandal."

Barb straightened her clipboard. "I prefer to think of it as preserving narrative tension."

Nanette closed the ledger carefully and set it on the table. "The next step is simple but important—we turn this over to the Historical Society and the county clerk. Then we make sure everyone knows the truth, publicly."

Matt nodded. "Already in motion. I've got the official statement drafted. The mayor's agreed to a press conference this afternoon."

"Perfect," I said. "Let's finally clear Eleanor's name once and for all."

By noon, word had already started spreading faster than a dropped tray of cinnamon rolls at Bunco night. The Morning Glory's porch became a revolving door of visitors—each with their own version of the story and at least one baked good.

Mavis Rigsby arrived first, clutching a plate of pecan bars and the latest issue of *The Marigold Gazette*. "Heard there's breaking news," she said, barely pausing for breath. "And you know, I've always said those Wexlers got a raw deal. Shame about Colton, though. He had such nice handwriting."

"Pecan bars to your left, justice to your right," Barb directed, ushering her toward the kitchen like an event planner for chaos.

By the time the mayor's car pulled into the driveway, there were at least a dozen townsfolk milling around the porch, sipping coffee, exchanging theories, and generally trying to look like they hadn't been waiting to eavesdrop.

Mayor Reed stepped out, hat in hand, his expression somber. "Miss Fisher, Detective Hale," he greeted. "I wanted to speak with you personally before the announcement. On behalf of the Reed family, I'd like to apologize—for everything."

"You don't have to apologize for the past," I said gently. "Just help us move forward."

He nodded. "That's exactly what I intend to do."

Hannah stood beside me, arms folded, her jaw set with quiet resolve. "You can start by making sure the Wexlers get a proper memorial at the Historical Society," she said. "And maybe a new sign on the old lumber mill—one with the right names this time."

The mayor looked at her, clearly taken aback by her steady tone. "Consider it done."

"Good," she said. "Then maybe we can finally stop pretending everything in this town is picture-perfect when it's really just a jigsaw puzzle missing half the pieces."

Barb scribbled that line on her notepad. "Excellent quote. I'm using it for next week's feature."

That afternoon, the town gathered outside the courthouse. The air was crisp, the sky a perfect autumn blue, and a faint scent of caramel apples drifted from the vendor on the corner. Marigold Lake had a way of turning even scandal into a social event.

Nanette stood near the steps, ledger in hand, while Matt and I flanked her. Hannah was there too, looking nervous but determined.

Mayor Reed stepped up to the podium. "My friends," he began, his voice wavering slightly, "for many years, this town has believed a lie. Today, that lie ends."

He nodded to Nanette, who opened the ledger and began to read. Her voice, clear and steady, carried across the square as she summarized the entries that proved Eleanor Wexler's innocence and Richard Reed's deception. Murmurs rippled through the crowd—shock, sorrow, and something else: relief.

When Nanette finished, there was a long, reverent silence. Then Mrs. Ainsworth dabbed her eyes with a lace handkerchief and announced, "Well, that settles it. I'll be dedicating this year's community play to Eleanor Wexler. Title: *The Truth Will Rise*."

"Make sure there's a good role for Sadie," I whispered to Matt.

"She's already been cast," Barb said, overhearing us. "As 'the conscience of Marigold Lake.'"

Sadie barked once, clearly approving.

The crowd slowly began to disperse, the tension melting into chatter about fall festivals and pie sales. Hannah stayed behind, gazing up at the courthouse steps.

"You okay?" I asked softly.

She nodded. "Yeah. It's strange, though. For years, I thought my family's story was about pride and respectability. Turns out it's about guilt and forgiveness. But maybe that's better. Feels more honest."

I smiled. "Honest suits you, Hannah. And for what it's worth, I think Aunt Teresa would've been proud of how you handled all this."

She smiled faintly. "You really think so?"

"I know so," I said. "She always said truth and kindness make the best recipe. Sometimes you just have to let them bake a little longer."

That evening, the Morning Glory felt lighter than it had in weeks. The kitchen smelled of cinnamon and apple pie, and laughter drifted through the dining room as friends gathered to celebrate the end of the storm.

Nanette was holding court by the fireplace, recounting her "daring archival triumph." Barb was taking down quotes for her article while simultaneously dishing out pie slices with military precision. Finn had arrived late, toolbelt still on, claiming he'd been "repairing emotional damage one fence at a time." Hannah swatted him with a dish towel.

Matt leaned against the counter beside me, mug in hand. "You did good, Claire," he said. "You brought the truth to light."

I shook my head. "We did good. You, me, Nanette, Hannah, and even Sadie."

At the mention of her name, Sadie trotted in from the hall, proudly dragging one of Matt's shoes.

"She's branching out from muffins to footwear," Matt said dryly.

"She's multi-talented," I replied.

He laughed, setting his mug down. "You know, I thought this treasure hunt would end in disaster."

"It nearly did," I said, thinking of the detonator, the dust, the sheer panic. "But it also gave us something better than gold."

"Proof?" he guessed.

"Peace," I said. "And a reason to keep baking."

He smiled, the kind that made me feel like home was wherever we happened to stand. "So what's next for Marigold Lake's favorite sleuth?"

"Laundry," I said with a grin. "And then maybe a new coat of paint on the porch swing before the snow comes."

Barb called out from across the room. "You forgot the part where you solve another mystery before Christmas!"

I rolled my eyes. "Let me enjoy one pie in peace first."

"Never gonna happen," she said. "This town can't go two weeks without drama."

She wasn't wrong.

Later that night, after everyone had gone home and the last dish was washed, I sat on the porch with a blanket around my shoulders and Sadie curled up beside me. The moon shimmered over the lake, casting silver ripples across the water.

Matt joined me, handing me a mug of tea. "For the record," he said, "I vote this is the last treasure hunt for a while."

"No promises," I said, smiling into my mug. "But if the next one involves less sabotage and more muffins, I'll consider it."

He chuckled, resting his arm along the back of the bench. "You think you'll ever stop chasing mysteries?"

"Probably not," I admitted. "But at least I'll always know who's got my back."

Sadie gave a small snort, which I took as agreement.

The lake was calm again. The ledger rested safely in Nanette's keeping, the town had its closure, and the Morning Glory glowed softly against the dark—steady, welcoming, full of second chances.

As the crickets sang and the wind rustled through the pines, I leaned my head on Matt's shoulder and whispered, "Truth endures."

Sadie yawned, curling tighter at our feet.

And for the first time in weeks, everything in Marigold Lake felt exactly as it should—imperfect, unpredictable, and wonderfully, beautifully home.

Chapter 23

Commitments and Confessions

If there was one thing I'd learned about life in Marigold Lake, it was that peace never arrived quietly. It came in bursts—like the pop of a champagne cork, the clatter of dishes at breakfast, or in this case, the loud clang of a dropped muffin tin.

Hannah groaned, bent to retrieve the pan, and muttered something that sounded suspiciously like, "If love doesn't kill me, baking will."

From my spot at the kitchen island, I smiled into my coffee. "That's quite a declaration for eight in the morning."

"Don't judge me," she said, brushing flour off her cheek. "Finn's coming by in, like, fifteen minutes, and I'm trying to bake apology muffins. Except I don't even know if we're in a fight. Are we in a fight?"

Sadie tilted her head, as if weighing in.

"I think the muffins are an excellent idea," I said. "But maybe consider that the sheer number of apology muffins you've made for Finn could open a small bakery."

Hannah sighed and slumped against the counter. "You're right. I just... I want him to know I'm serious this time. That I'm done with the mixed signals and accidental ghosting and 'let's take a break because I panicked over matching flannel shirts.'"

I bit back a laugh. "Ah yes, the great flannel crisis of last winter."

Her cheeks pinked. "He said it made us look like an ad for maple syrup."

Sadie barked once, which I chose to interpret as accurate.

I reached over and squeezed her hand. "You care about him, Hannah. That's obvious to everyone except, apparently, you two. Maybe stop baking your feelings and just tell him."

Her eyes widened. "Like, words?"

"Radical concept, I know."

She smiled, nervous but genuine. "Maybe you're right. I'll talk to him. After I frost these."

Finn arrived exactly fourteen minutes later, toolbelt slung over his shoulder and a cautious smile on his face. "Morning," he said, his voice as warm as the sunlight streaming through the kitchen windows. "Smells good in here. Is that forgiveness or just breakfast?"

"Maybe both," Hannah said, sliding the plate of muffins toward him.

He picked one up, examined it like evidence, then looked at her. "So... peace offering?"

"More like olive branch," she said. "With cinnamon."

He chuckled, but there was tension in the air—the kind that hung around two people trying to say everything without saying it. I took my cue to disappear, scooping up Sadie and heading for the porch.

"Come on, detective," I whispered to her. "Let's give them some privacy."

Sadie grumbled softly but followed, hopping into her usual spot by the window. I left the door cracked—purely for airflow, of course.

Inside, voices drifted out in uneven rhythms—murmurs, pauses, a laugh that broke the tension. Then came silence. And then... the sound of Finn's low voice saying something I couldn't make out, followed by Hannah's breathless laugh that told me whatever he'd said was exactly right.

When I peeked in again a few minutes later, Finn's hand was covering hers across the table. Her face glowed in a way that had nothing to do with the oven.

"Well," I said, stepping inside, "I take it the muffins worked."

Hannah beamed. "We talked. Like, really talked. And we're done playing the guessing game."

"Congratulations," I said. "Does this mean I can stop stocking emergency ice cream for your emotional emergencies?"

She threw a dish towel at me. "You love being part of the drama."

"Only as an observer," I said, dodging it. "I like my chaos in manageable doses."

Finn grinned. "You mean like electrical fires, runaway guests, and buried treasure?"

"Exactly."

He shifted, glancing at Hannah with a look that could melt frosting. "We're going to take a drive up to Willow Creek this afternoon. Talk about maybe... finding a place."

"Like a getaway?" I asked.

He hesitated, then said quietly, "Like something more permanent."

My eyebrows rose. "Well, that's one way to make sure you never have to schedule a Bunco night around leaky pipes again."

Hannah's blush deepened, but she didn't look away from him. "It's not official or anything," she said, "but we just want to see what's out there. Together."

I smiled, genuine and full. "You two deserve a fresh start."

Sadie barked twice—her version of approval.

Finn knelt and scratched behind her ears. "You hear that, Sadie? Big changes."

She licked his hand, which was as good as an endorsement.

By late afternoon, the B&B had settled into its familiar rhythm—the clink of teacups, the hum of conversation from the dining room, and Nanette bustling through the hall with a vase of wildflowers.

"Love is in the air," she said, setting the flowers down with a satisfied sigh. "Or maybe it's just the smell of banana bread."

"Could be both," I said. "Hannah and Finn seem to be moving forward."

"Oh, wonderful," Nanette said. "I was starting to worry she'd end up adopting another cat just to fill the emotional void."

"Sadie would've staged a coup," I said.

Nanette chuckled. "Well, tell them congratulations. But also remind them that if they move out, they're required to come back for Sunday breakfast. Emotional support pancakes are part of this household."

"Noted."

She gave me a sly look. "And what about you and Detective Hale? Any progress there?"

I tried to play it cool. "Progress?"

Nanette arched an eyebrow. "Claire, dear, I've seen the way you two look at each other. The only thing thicker than this town's gossip is your mutual denial."

"Subtle as always," I said dryly.

"I call it like I see it," she said, winking. "Now, don't mind me. I'm off to inventory the preserves before Barb's replacement guest eats them all."

As she bustled away, I turned to find Matt leaning in the doorway, coffee in hand and that familiar half-smile on his face.

"You know," he said, "I think Nanette's applying to be a licensed matchmaker."

"She'd have the market cornered," I said.

He chuckled and crossed the room, setting his mug down. "So, Hannah and Finn are finally on the same page?"

"Looks that way," I said. "And before you ask—no, I didn't eavesdrop. Much."

He grinned. "Good to know. You think they'll actually move forward?"

"I do," I said. "And I'm happy for them. They deserve it."

He nodded thoughtfully. "It's nice, seeing things work out for people around here. Makes you think about what's next."

There was a weight to his words—a soft, almost hesitant edge that made my heart skip.

"Next?" I echoed.

He glanced out the window toward the lake. "You ever think about that? What's next for you?"

"Constantly," I said. "But every time I try to plan ahead, the universe drops a missing ledger, a sabotaged bake sale, or a mysterious Boston Terrier clue in my lap."

"Maybe that's what keeps things interesting," he said.

"Maybe," I agreed.

We stood there for a moment, the sunlight slanting across the kitchen tiles, the smell of baking filling the air, and the quiet between us both comfortable and full of possibility.

That evening, Hannah and Finn returned from their drive, hand in hand and glowing like they'd discovered the meaning of life—or at least a really good real estate listing.

"Well?" I asked, meeting them on the porch. "Did you find anything promising?"

Finn nodded. "A little cottage near the north end of town. Needs work, but... it feels right."

"It has a garden," Hannah added. "And enough space for Finn's tools and my baking disasters."

Sadie trotted over to sniff their shoes, then barked as if approving their choice.

"Sounds perfect," I said. "Just make sure you keep a guest room open. I have a feeling we'll need it sooner or later."

"You think the Morning Glory might get too quiet without us?" Hannah teased.

"Never," I said. "But you'll always be family here. You and Finn—and anyone else who wanders into our chaos."

She smiled and hugged me tightly. "Thank you, Claire. For everything."

"Just promise me you'll invite me to the housewarming," I said. "And that you'll let me bring muffins."

"Deal," she said, laughing.

As they walked down the path, the evening sky painted in streaks of pink and gold, I felt a warmth settle in my chest. Hannah had found her footing. Finn had found someone who believed in him. And maybe, just maybe, Marigold Lake was finally beginning to heal from all its buried secrets.

Sadie pressed against my leg, her gaze following them until they disappeared around the corner. I reached down and scratched her head.

"You know, girl," I said softly, "for a town that claims to be sleepy, we sure keep busy."

She snorted, which I took as agreement.

The porch light flicked on, the first star blinked above the lake, and for a brief, perfect moment, all was right at the Morning Glory.

Chapter 24

Back to Normal

PEACE, I DECIDED, HAD a very particular sound at the Morning Glory.

It was the faint plink of a spoon stirring tea, the low hum of Nanette singing along to the radio, and the rhythmic click of Sadie's nails as she patrolled the hallway like the inn's four-legged security system.

After the chaos of the treasure hunt, the B&B had finally settled back into its normal rhythm—or, at least, Marigold Lake's version of normal, which always came with a touch of eccentricity.

"Claire, dear, the couple in Room Three wants to know if they can borrow a metal detector," Nanette called from the front desk. "Apparently, they lost a lucky penny in the garden."

I laughed, wiping my hands on a dish towel. "A lucky penny in our garden? It might never want to be found again."

Nanette's glasses slid down her nose as she peered at me over the counter. "Should I tell them we only loan out shovels and optimism?"

"Perfect," I said. "Throw in a cup of coffee and call it customer service."

Sadie trotted by with something suspiciously shiny in her mouth. I crouched down and gently pried it from her jaws—it was, of course, the missing penny.

"Sadie Fisher," I scolded. "You've been treasure hunting again."

Her nub tail wagged in proud defiance.

"Add 'finder of fortunes' to her résumé," Nanette said, grinning. "Honestly, that dog's done more for tourism than the entire Chamber of Commerce."

I pocketed the penny and headed for the garden. The air was cool and fresh, the kind of crisp autumn day that felt like a reward for surviving small-town scandal. The lake shimmered in the distance, framed by gold and amber trees. For the first time in weeks, I could breathe without worrying about who might turn up next with a clue, a confession, or a casserole.

Back in the dining room, the tables were full. The morning guests—a blend of familiar faces and a few curious newcomers—chattered over coffee and cinnamon scones.

At one table, Mrs. Ainsworth was holding court, dramatically recounting her "brush with danger" from the treasure hunt, which, according to her, involved coded letters, two near-death experiences, and one perfectly timed Shakespearean monologue.

"I simply told him," she said, gesturing grandly, "'The truth will out, though it be buried beneath deceit!'"

The young couple sitting across from her looked both dazzled and mildly alarmed.

Nanette leaned in and whispered to me, "If she starts quoting *Macbeth*, I'm confiscating her teapot."

At another table, Harold the postman was showing photos of his new kitten, which apparently "helped sort the mail by pawing at anything marked urgent."

And near the window, a quiet older man was sketching the lake in a leather-bound notebook, pausing occasionally to sip his tea. I'd learned he was an author passing through—Mr. Grayson, soft-spoken, kind, and entirely too interested in Sadie's detective career.

"She has excellent instincts," he'd said, scratching behind her ears. "Perhaps I'll make her the heroine of my next mystery."

Sadie, naturally, approved.

I carried out a tray of muffins and paused to soak in the scene. For all the chaos and heartbreak that had swept through Marigold Lake lately, this was what I loved most—the way people gathered, shared, and healed here. The Morning Glory wasn't just a bed-and-breakfast. It was a second chance for anyone who walked through its doors.

Nanette joined me, holding two steaming mugs of cider. "For you," she said, handing one over. "And before you ask—yes, I used Aunt Teresa's recipe. The one that tastes like fall and forgiveness."

"High praise," I said, taking a sip. "And accurate. You know, Nanette, sometimes I think the Morning Glory runs better without me."

She gave me a pointed look. "Don't say that, Claire. You're the heartbeat of this place. Without you, it's just a building full of biscuits."

"Flattering," I said with a laugh.

She softened. "You brought everyone together after all that nonsense with the treasure hunt. People trust you here. That's not something you can bake into a muffin."

I felt a lump in my throat, and for a moment, all I could manage was, "Thanks, Nanette."

She winked. "Besides, someone has to keep Matt Hale from brooding himself into oblivion."

As if summoned by name, Matt appeared in the doorway, his jacket dusted with the crisp scent of autumn. Sadie barked once and bounded to him, tail vibrating with delight.

"Afternoon, ladies," he said, giving me that familiar half-smile that still managed to unsettle every coherent thought in my head. "Smells good in here."

"Cinnamon and redemption," Nanette quipped. "Want some cider, Detective?"

"Don't mind if I do," he said, taking a mug.

He leaned against the counter, his gaze settling on me. "You look less stressed. That's a good sign."

"I'm trying to adjust to the radical idea of peace and quiet," I said. "It's unsettling."

He chuckled. "You'll get used to it. Though knowing this town, probably not for long."

Nanette raised her mug. "To Marigold Lake: where peace is seasonal."

We clinked cups in agreement.

By mid-afternoon, the guests began drifting out to enjoy the lakeside trails. Nanette tidied the counter while I stacked plates and Sadie supervised from a chair, chin on paws, eyes half-closed.

"That's the look of a dog who's solved one too many mysteries," I said.

Nanette chuckled. "She's earned her nap. So have you, dear."

"Tempting," I said, glancing toward the porch. "But I might take my coffee outside instead."

"Go on," she said. "Before the next round of chaos arrives."

I stepped outside, the screen door creaking softly behind me. The porch was bathed in warm sunlight, the lake gleaming beyond. Across the yard, Hannah and Finn were sitting on the stone wall, their heads close together as they studied a folded brochure—real-estate listings, no doubt.

It made me smile. They looked happy. Steady. Like two people who'd finally figured out which direction their compass pointed.

Matt joined me a few minutes later, his footsteps quiet on the porch boards. "They look good together," he said.

"They do," I agreed. "It's nice to see something in this town turn out simple for once."

He chuckled softly. "You're telling me."

We stood in companionable silence for a while, sipping our coffee and watching as the afternoon sun shimmered on the lake.

After a moment, he said, "You ever think about taking a break, Claire? Maybe getting away for a while? You've earned it."

I tilted my head. "You offering to handle the guest check-ins while I'm gone?"

He smirked. "Let's not get carried away."

"I didn't think so," I said with a grin. "Anyway, if I left, who would stop Barb's replacement from redecorating with plastic pumpkins in July?"

"Good point," he said. "But seriously—if you ever need to breathe, you should. The town will survive for a few days without you."

"Maybe," I said, taking a slow sip. "But I think I'd miss it too much. The noise. The people. Even the chaos."

He glanced at me, his eyes soft. "Yeah," he said quietly. "Me too."

Later, as the sun dipped low and guests trickled back for dinner, I found myself in the kitchen again—baking, of course. There was something about mixing flour and sugar that made the world feel orderly again. Sadie curled at my feet, tail flicking whenever a crumb dared fall within her reach.

Nanette hummed along to a tune from the radio. Matt set out extra plates because, as he said, "Someone always shows up uninvited in this town."

Hannah and Finn arrived just as the timer dinged, carrying a basket of apples from the farmer's market.

"For the next round of baking disasters," Hannah announced.

"You mean experiments," Finn corrected.

"Same thing," she said, laughing.

The warmth, the laughter, the scent of baked apples—it all wrapped around me like the coziest quilt imaginable.

This was home.

And for the first time in a long while, it truly felt like one.

That night, as the guests retired and Nanette turned off the front light, I lingered on the porch. Sadie hopped onto the swing beside me, curling up against my hip. The moon glowed silver over the lake, its reflection rippling like an old secret finally at peace.

"Another mystery solved, girl," I whispered. "Let's try not to find another one for a few weeks, okay?"

Sadie sighed, the contented kind that meant "no promises."

I smiled. "Didn't think so."

Chapter 25

The Porch at Sunset

Evening came softly to Marigold Lake. The last of the sunlight caught on the water, scattering gold like spilled honey, and the porch of the Morning Glory seemed to glow from within.

Nanette had declared it "a porch supper evening," and that was that. Within an hour, we'd conjured up a table that groaned under the weight of fried chicken, cornbread, peach cobbler, and about six kinds of salads that all mysteriously contained either pasta or mayonnaise.

The scent of warm biscuits drifted through the air, mingling with laughter and the rhythmic creak of the old porch swing.

Sadie sat at my feet wearing a red-and-white bandana that said **Chief Investigator**, which Hannah had embroidered that afternoon. Every so often, she'd lift her head and sniff the air longingly, clearly convinced her invitation to the dinner table had been lost in the mail.

"Claire, if you don't give that dog a biscuit soon, she's going to file a complaint," Matt said, balancing his plate on his knee.

"She already did," I said. "It's the stare-down phase of negotiations."

Sadie huffed as if to prove my point.

Hannah laughed from her spot across the table, her arm looped comfortably through Finn's. "You two are hopeless," she said. "Also, I might have made Sadie a peach-cobbler sample. For, you know, quality control."

Finn raised an eyebrow. "Is that what you're calling it now?"

"Better than emotional eating," she shot back.

Nanette clucked her tongue. "Emotional eating is perfectly respectable. I've been doing it since 1978 and I've never once regretted a cobbler."

Everyone laughed. The sound rippled across the porch, mixing with the gentle buzz of crickets and the low rustle of wind through the trees. For the first time in what felt like ages, there was no tension, no mystery pressing on my shoulders—just the soft, golden comfort of being home.

After dinner, Matt helped Nanette clear the table while Hannah and Finn brought out coffee and pie. Mrs. Ainsworth had stopped by "just to drop off leftover shortbread," but somehow she'd ended up in the rocking chair, recounting her *pivotal role* in the treasure hunt yet again.

"And of course," she said, gesturing grandly with her coffee cup, "when I told Colton Parrish that deceit would never prosper, I knew I'd struck fear into his heart!"

Finn leaned close to Hannah and whispered, "Pretty sure what struck fear into him was her trying to quote Shakespeare while brandishing a spatula."

Hannah snorted into her pie.

I caught Matt's eye and grinned. "Think we should warn her that she's in danger of being written into Mr. Grayson's next mystery novel?"

"Let's see how many scenes she writes herself into first," he murmured back.

Sadie let out a sigh and flopped across my feet, perfectly content. The breeze stirred the curtains, carrying with it the faintest whiff of cinnamon and lake water.

It was perfect.

Nanette reappeared with her knitting basket, announcing that she was "multi-tasking—conversation and productivity." Finn was tuning an old guitar someone had brought from the parlor. Hannah had propped her feet up on the railing, humming along softly.

"This," she said, "is what happiness looks like."

"You said that about finding a cottage with working plumbing," Finn teased.

"Plumbing *is* happiness," she countered.

Matt chuckled. "I can't argue with that logic."

I smiled, taking it all in. "You know," I said, "if you'd told me a few months ago that a centuries-old family feud, a treasure hunt, and an accidental hostage situation would lead to this porch dinner, I'd have said you were crazy."

"Only in Marigold Lake," Hannah said dreamily.

"Exactly," I agreed. "It's unpredictable. Messy. Completely charming."

Nanette glanced up from her knitting. "That should be the town motto."

"Can we put it on the welcome sign?" Finn asked. "Right next to the one that says *Population: fluctuating depending on gossip*."

Everyone laughed again, and I felt that deep, quiet joy that comes when the world finally rights itself.

Matt leaned closer, lowering his voice. "You did good, Claire."

I tilted my head. "How do you mean?"

"Everything," he said simply. "You held this town together. You found the truth when everyone else was chasing shadows. You have a way of seeing people—not just their mistakes, but who they are underneath."

The words caught me off guard. "That's... quite possibly the nicest thing anyone's ever said to me," I said softly.

"Get used to it," he said with a grin.

Our eyes met, and for a heartbeat, the noise around us faded. Then Sadie barked, effectively ruining the moment.

Matt laughed. "She's jealous."

"She just wants attention," I said. "Or dessert."

Sadie thumped her paw against my foot as if to confirm both.

Later, after the dishes were done and most of the guests had gone to bed, only a handful of us remained on the porch. The air had turned cool, the stars bright enough to reflect on the still surface of the lake.

Hannah leaned her head on Finn's shoulder, Nanette dozed off mid-knit, and Mrs. Ainsworth had finally, mercifully run out of dialogue.

Matt stood by the railing, gazing out at the water. I joined him, the boards creaking softly beneath my steps.

"Beautiful night," I said.

He nodded. "Peaceful."

"Almost too peaceful," I said. "I'm half-expecting someone to call about a missing pie or a stolen lawn gnome."

He smiled. "You say that like it's a bad thing."

"Depends on the pie," I said.

He looked at me for a long moment, then said quietly, "I'm glad you're here, Claire. Really."

I felt my heart skip. "Right back at you, Detective."

Sadie gave a sleepy bark from her blanket by the door, as if punctuating the sentiment.

The moon climbed higher, painting everything silver. The lake lapped softly at the shore, and the porch light flickered like a heartbeat.

"Hey," Hannah said suddenly, sitting up straighter. "Did anyone else hear that?"

We all turned. From somewhere down the road came a faint clang. Then another.

"Relax," Nanette murmured without opening her eyes. "Probably just Harold locking up the post office again. He never remembers which key is which."

Still, something in the sound made me smile. It wasn't ominous—just familiar. The kind of sound that said life goes on, even after secrets are uncovered and mysteries are solved.

Matt brushed a hand over my shoulder. "You're thinking about the next one already, aren't you?"

"Maybe," I admitted. "It's hard not to. This town practically breeds intrigue."

He grinned. "Good thing you're around to handle it."

I laughed softly. "We'll see. For now, I'm perfectly happy with quiet evenings, scones that don't contain clues, and dogs that only dig for bones, not evidence."

Sadie groaned as if to say *no promises.*

As the night deepened, conversation dwindled to contented silence. The last candle flickered out, and the stars above Marigold Lake seemed impossibly bright.

I leaned back in the swing, watching the ripples on the water. For all its quirks, this town had become my anchor. My mystery. My home.

Tomorrow there would be new guests, new gossip, and—if I was being honest—probably another secret waiting to surface. But for now, I had everything I needed: friends, peace, and one very sleepy Boston Terrier snoring softly against my knee.

I reached down and scratched her head. "You did good, girl."

Her tail twitched.

The night air was cool, the world was quiet, and all was well at the Morning Glory.

At least until next time.

Epilogue

The Quiet Between Mysteries

THE LAST OF THE tourists had gone home. Marigold Lake had slipped into that golden lull between autumn bustle and winter chill—the kind of quiet that felt like an exhale after a long, dramatic chapter.

From the porch of the Morning Glory, I watched the water shimmer in the fading light. The maples had shed most of their leaves, carpeting the ground in orange and gold. Sadie snored beside me, curled into a tight little ball, her nub tail twitching with every dream.

Nanette called it "restorative silence," though she'd immediately broken it that morning by announcing she was reorganizing the linen closet "for morale."

I didn't mind the quiet. After everything—the treasure hunt, Colton Parrish, the scandal that rattled half the town—stillness felt like a luxury.

Inside, the kettle whistled. I poured myself a cup of tea, the scent of chamomile and cinnamon filling the air, and returned to the porch. For once, the only mysteries demanding my attention were whether Sadie would wake up for dinner and whether Nanette's idea of "organizing" meant alphabetizing pillowcases again.

The town was healing. The Wexler name had been cleared, Hannah and Finn were setting up their new cottage near Willow Creek, and Matt had almost stopped raising an eyebrow every time the phone rang—*almost.*

He showed up just after sunset, hands tucked in his jacket pockets, that familiar look of quiet concern shadowing his face.

"Evening, Detective," I said. "I thought you'd be busy keeping Mrs. Ainsworth from reporting another 'ghost sighting' in her garden."

He chuckled. "Already handled it. Turned out to be Harold's new cat."

"Poor cat. Probably traumatized."

He leaned against the porch railing, eyes sweeping over the lake. "It's quiet tonight."

"Too quiet?" I teased.

"Just right," he said, smiling faintly. "I was thinking we should enjoy it while it lasts."

"That sounds suspiciously like foreshadowing."

He gave me a look that said *you're probably right.*

Sadie stirred, let out a soft snort, and rolled onto her back, paws in the air. Matt laughed quietly. "I think she's got the right idea. You should try that—relaxing."

"I'm working on it," I said. "Though I admit, part of me keeps expecting something strange to happen."

"This is Marigold Lake," he said. "Something strange *always* happens."

"True," I said, taking a sip of tea. "But maybe not tonight."

We sat there for a while, the silence companionable, the world still. The porch light flickered once, casting a warm glow on the steps, and an owl called somewhere in the woods.

For the first time in months, I felt entirely at peace.

The next morning dawned crisp and bright. I woke early, baked a batch of Morning Glory Muffins, and opened the front door just as the first rays of sunlight hit the lake.

That's when I saw it.

A small package sat neatly on the porch, tied with twine. No name, no return address. Just a simple note attached:

"For the Keeper of Memories."

My stomach did a slow flip.

I knelt and picked it up, the paper cool beneath my fingers. Sadie trotted over, sniffing eagerly, her tail wagging.

"Not food, girl," I murmured, though my heart was already racing.

Matt appeared at the top of the stairs, coffee in hand. "Please tell me that's from the mailman and not another mystery."

"Too early to tell," I said, eyeing the handwriting. "But I have a bad feeling Harold didn't deliver this."

He joined me, studying the package. "You going to open it?"

"Eventually," I said. "Maybe after breakfast."

He smirked. "You said that last time."

"That was different," I said. "That time involved potential explosives."

Sadie barked once, sharply, as if urging me to stop stalling.

"Fine," I said, untying the twine. Inside was a small wooden box, smooth and worn, with a faint scent of cedar. I lifted the lid slowly.

Nestled inside was a single object: a brass key. Old-fashioned, ornate, its bow shaped like a heart.

I turned it over, squinting in the morning light. Two letters were etched into the metal.

W.H.

"Wexler House," Matt murmured. "You think it's connected?"

"Or a coincidence," I said, though I didn't believe that for a second.

Sadie let out another bark and trotted toward the path that led to the garden—toward the very direction of the old Wexler estate.

I sighed. "Looks like peace and quiet were short-lived."

Matt smiled. "You are sure you're up for another mystery?"

I tucked the key into my pocket and glanced at Sadie, who was already on alert, tail wagging like a metronome.

"I was born for it," I said. "Besides, someone has to keep this town interesting."

He grinned. "You do that just fine."

The sun rose higher, glinting off the lake, turning everything gold. I looked out over Marigold Lake—my home, my chaos, my heart—and felt that familiar spark of curiosity light up again.

The quiet was over.

And that was perfectly fine by me.

About Reva Davenport

Reva Davenport is the author of the *Marigold Lake Cozy Mystery* series, where small-town secrets, humor, and heart-warming friendship collide. Her stories follow Claire Fisher—a quick-witted bed-and-breakfast owner—and her Boston Terrier, Sadie, as they uncover mysteries and mischief in the charming lakeside town of Marigold Lake, Iowa.

When Reva isn't writing about cinnamon-scented kitchens, tangled clues, and community chaos, she can be found baking new recipes, designing cozy bookplates, or enjoying quiet moments with a good cup of coffee and a mischievous pup for company.

You can connect with Reva, join her *Scones, Secrets & Sleuths* reader team, or sign up for her newsletter at revadavenport.com for exclusive updates and sneak peeks at upcoming books.

Also by Reva Davenport

<u>A MARIGOLD LAKE COZY MYSTERY SERIES</u>

Secrets Buried in the Backyard

Dead Air at the Morning Glory

The Suitcase at the Morning Glory

Flour Power at the Morning Glory

The Missing Brooch at the Morning Glory

My Sister at the Morning Glory

Christmas at the Morning Glory

Treasure at the Morning Glory

**<u>And more cozy mysteries from Marigold Lake coming
soon!</u>**

Coming Soon From Reva Davenport

The Valentine Vendetta at the Morning Glory   **Arriving December 26, 2025**

Love is in the air... and so is mischief. When a Valentine's Day celebration at the Morning Glory takes a turn for the mysterious,
Claire Fisher and her Boston Terrier, Sadie, must follow the trail of heart-shaped chaos before romance turns into ruin.